Christmas in '45
A Novel

Mark W Sasse

Contact the Author

www.mwsasse.com
Email: Mark@mwsasse.com
Facebook: www.facebook.com/markwsasse

CONTENTS

Chapter 1

Christmas Eve '44

Roberta soared through the house. Room to room. Kitchen. Dining room. Living room. Laughing as she squeezed a wooden spoon in her hand, cross ways, like she pushed the wing of an airplane into the stratosphere. Her mouth hummed a steady rumble of an engine in flight, and she kept one pace ahead of Trigger, the terrier, nipping and barking at her heels in playful delight.

"Hmmmmm. Whooosh!"

"Roberta!"

She sailed past her mother's ear like a gale force wind, nearly causing her mother to spill a pot of raw eggnog she balanced in her hands.

"Roberta! Be careful!"

"Whooooo … Trigger. To the tree. Climb to the star of the tree. That's what planes do. They soar to the stars."

She jumped on top of a stool next to the Christmas tree and reached as high as she could until the make-believe, wooden spoon plane zigzagged past the star on top of the medium-sized cut pine.

"Mom! Can I have a string of popcorn?"

"No. Don't touch the tree. The Dwyers are coming over tonight."

"Can I have just a little?"

"Not one kernel."

"Mom!"

"Roberta. I'm busy here."

"So am I. I'm learning to fly like daddy. Do you think he'll send me a real model airplane for Christmas?"

"We'll see if he got word to Santa."

"Mom, I don't believe in Santa."

"Why would you say that?"

"Because airplanes fly for real, but reindeer can't fly."

"Christmas magic makes them fly. This is the season for miracles, Roberta."

"Mom, only planes fly. And birds."

"What about wooden spoons?"

"Mom! It's the only thing I got. I don't have a real model airplane. Remember how daddy used to fly our silverware around the table during dinner."

Roberta made another flyover through the kitchen.

"I never appreciated that."

"I did. It proves that anything can fly if you wish it."

"So then reindeer can fly?"

"No, Mom. Don't be silly." She flew past the tree and plopped onto the sofa knee first, arms resting on the back of the cushion, and looked out the picture window into the snowy evening to watch flurries sparkling in the lights. "Can I please take a string of popcorn off the tree?"

"No!"

"Mom …"

"Roberta, stop whining."

"Mom …"

"Roberta!"

"Mom. There's someone coming to the door. They're wearing uniforms."

A loud sound echoed from the kitchen. A metal banging. Roberta twirled around but couldn't see what happened. Her mother said nothing, and the air in the room seemed to pause for a second, like the marrow of the moment had been sucked dry, like life was stiff and brittle.

Knock. Three of them. Bare knuckled on the wood. Roberta ran to the door and flung it open. In front of her stood two men, who looked like daddy, three-buttoned brown jacket. Stripes on both arms which formed an A without the cross bar. Shiny small colored squares clung to the left breast of both of the airmen. And a bird, with wings spread right above the shiny squares. Roberta almost jumped into one of their arms thinking that … But the face didn't match. She stared for a moment. Puzzled. She had never seen a uniform like this around there. Only the photos of daddy. The two men, standing shoulder to shoulder, removed their caps and placed them under their left arms. They wore no expressions, and Roberta thought they didn't look friendly. Why would they be here on Christmas Eve? One spoke.

"Is your mother home?"

"Yes, she—"

Roberta felt her mother's hand on her arm. There was a tug, a quick one, pulling Roberta backward. She glanced up and saw her mother holding a dish towel nearly covering her face. Her voice cracked.

"Roberta. Go upstairs."

"Mom, what's going on?"

"Go upstairs." She pushed her backwards, and almost tripped over Trigger. Roberta scooped the dog into her arms and ran up the stairs like her mother said. But not the whole way. She stopped halfway at the landing, curious, lost in the eyes of the two men staring glumly at her mother, who leaned against the door frame.

"Mrs. Ares?"

That's all they said. She collapsed on the floor to her knees, the dish towel covering her entire face, but it couldn't muffle the sounds of the weeping. Loud. Wailing. Each audible breath like a pin prick in Roberta's ear, telling her of trouble, but not explaining it. Roberta's chest constricted like she was suffocating, and she cried too, for her mother, for her acquaintance with grief which visited her for the first time in the form of two soldiers. She held Trigger in a full body hug and waited for answers.

The two men squatted. Each putting one of their hands on the grieving mother's shoulders. The wind whipped through the open door. Whisks of snow blew into the living room and disappeared as droplets against the warm air. Roberta heard words. Whispers. They were like breaths of the winter wind, sailing from tree to tree, informing the forest of the incoming storm. Prepare. The attack awaits. Ready the wings. You'll need them to fly to safety.

After a few moments, frozen in fear, courage rose and she spoke once.

"Mom?"

The grieving wife let out a sigh, and turned towards her daughter. She reached for her, motioning for her to come. Roberta released

Trigger onto the steps, and she ran to her and felt a hug like no other. It had nothing to do with *I love you* or *Goodnight;* this was a hug of intensity. The tears mingled into her brown hair, and they held each other. Trigger whimpered in the middle of them.

"What's wrong?"

Her mother stood and grabbed Roberta's arm. She walked her into the living room. The two airmen closed the door and followed.

"Here, please sit."

"No, ma'am. It's alright."

"Please. Have a seat. Could I get you some spiced cider?"

"No, ma'am. We could come back if it would be better. We're so sorry to intrude on Christmas Eve."

"No, please. Sit."

She motioned to the sofa, and the two men sat in tandem. Mother sat across from them on a swivel, high-back chair with Roberta on her lap.

"Roberta." Her mother had collected herself and spoke in a strong voice. "These men came with some bad news about your father. He has died, Roberta. In the war. I'm so sorry."

Died. The word had meaning. Some. It meant he would never come back. He would never cross the lake back to her. That's what he had called it.

She remembered. The lake. But she had lived without him for two years already. He was always far away, and now too he was far away. It didn't feel different. Or real. But she saw her mother's tears. Those were real. She remembered them from the funeral of Grandpa Newsom last year, and he never visited them again. Though they had visited the cemetery a time or two. She recalled the large stone with the words carved into it. *Would daddy have a stone like that? Is that where I will visit him, beside Grandpa Newsom?* No, it can't be. *I don't want to visit Daddy there. Daddy promised me he'd come back. He would bring me an airplane. Not a real one. A model one. That looked just like the one he flew.* Her thoughts formed into a question, which she asked to the two men.

"Is Daddy still across the lake?"

They didn't understand.

"Can you tell me what happened?" her mother asked.

"In front of the child?"

"Just tell us."

"Very well, ma'am."

There were many words she didn't understand. Died kept ringing in her ears. She thought of her daddy taking her down to the lake, right across the street, and telling her what it would be like. Plane went down. She heard that.

And she knew what happened when a plane crashed. She was far away from the conversation when she heard her name.

"Roberta, her name is Roberta."

"Roberta," spoke one of the officers, "your daddy is a hero. I have something for you." He unpinned the wings from his jacket and reached across a coffee table to hand it to her. "Here. Take this. These wings will keep alive the memories of your father. Allow them to fly. Never hide them. Know that your father was a hero."

"Did my daddy have wings, too?"

"That's right, sweetheart. Wings of angels. Now you both have them."

Her mother could barely speak. She mouthed a "thank you" under her breath.

"Is there anything we can do for you, ma'am?"

"No, thank you."

"You won't be alone here?"

"No, we have friends and family coming. Thank you."

"Our sincere condolences to you and your daughter. From all accounts, your husband was an honorable and good man."

"Yes, yes he was."

The men left. The two sat dazed staring into the fire. Her mother told her to take a string of popcorn off the tree. Roberta did, and she munched on the kernels as she stared at the metal airplane pin in her hand.

Chapter 2

Across the Lake

The sun shone deep and long as the evening rays painted the silhouettes of sprawling trees onto the green, like monsters with stretched limbs trying to claim as much land as possible with every inch of each bony twig. Roberta and her father walked hand in hand on the tips of the shadows, across the street, towards the lake, which lay ahead as a sheen expanse of tranquility.

"I like your uniform, Daddy."

"Why, thank you. That's what I want to talk to you about."

As soon as they crossed the street, Roberta took off running toward the water only a narrow patch of grass away. Her father ran after her, joking he would catch her. She screamed in delight, and they both rolled and curled up on the matted green grass in front of a hundred-year-old oak, standing as a watchtower of the body of water which helped define the entire community.

"Daddy, look at the boat."

"A sailboat."

"I wanna go on a sailboat."

"I'll take you one day."

"A caterpillar." The insect distracted Roberta, and she scooped it into her hands and displayed it with proud conviction. "It's soft."

"Yes, it is." He watched her. A content smile on his face. "Roberta, I want to tell you something."

"What? Can I name the caterpillar?"

"Sure."

"What should I name it?"

"Something beautiful because it's going to turn into a butterfly."

"How about Mommy? I'll name it Mommy, cause Mommy's beautiful, isn't she Daddy?"

He laughed. "She's the most beautiful woman, and she has the most beautiful daughter. You." He poked her in the side and picked her up into his lap.

"Listen, Roberta, I'm wearing the uniform today because I have to tell you something."

"What?" she asked, head cocked down as she petted the caterpillar.

"Daddy's going away."

"Where?"

"Far away. I have to fly an airplane for our country."

She looked up at him with a puzzled stare.

"You already fly airplanes, Daddy."

"That's right. Remember when I took you to the airport and we walked around to see the planes?"

"They're so big and they go … vrooom into the sky." Both of them said that in unison. "Vroom. Vroom."

They each mimicked a plane in flight. Her father's hand came in for a landing and tickled her. The laugh echoed onto the water.

"Now the country needs me to help them, and to fly airplanes for the army. That's why I'm wearing this uniform. I need to help the country. It's very important, so I'm going to be far away."

"When will you come back?"

"It will be a long time."

Roberta paused for a moment. She remembered having to wait for her birthday when she turned seven, and she asked if it would be that long. Like waiting for a birthday.

"Much longer, because the place I'm going is very far away."

"Where is it?"

"That's why I wanted to bring you down to the lake. Look out across the water. How big is it?"

"It's huge! Bigger than our house."

"Much bigger. I'm going to be traveling over

water, like this lake, but even much bigger. And I'm going to be on the other side of the water. And I'll be flying airplanes to help the soldiers, to help the men in uniform. And as soon as I'm finished, I'll come back from across the water, and we'll be together again."

She thought about being far away. "It's like Christmas cards."

"What do you mean?"

"When people are far away, and you can't see them, you send them Christmas cards. That's what Mommy says. Then we remember them."

"That's right, Roberta. But don't worry, I'll send you more than just Christmas cards. I'll write to you all the time. And you'll write to me, won't you?"

"Yes, Daddy."

He hugged her. "That will make me so happy. You know what, when you come down to the lake, I want you to think about me. Here."

He stood up and held her in his arms. He walked to the edge of the water.

"Look. Look way on the other side of the lake. When you come down here, promise me that when you look across the water and see the other side that you'll think of me, and say hi to me. You'll know in your heart that I'm thinking of you and missing you so much. All right, you promise?"

"I promise. And Daddy."

"Yes, sweetheart."

"I'll pray for you when I go to bed."

He kissed her on the forehead. "Thank you, Roberta."

He placed her on the ground and put his hand on his chin in a deep-in-thought pose.

"You know, Roberta. I've been thinking. It's just gonna be you and mommy in the house with me gone, and I was trying to think of a way so you both wouldn't be so lonely. Hmm. I have an idea. Follow me."

He took off running along the edge of the lake. Roberta bolted after him.

"You can't catch me."

"Yes, I can."

"This way, this way. I have a great idea."

"Daddy!"

"Over here."

He hid behind a tree and jumped out at her as she passed by. She screamed and he laughed and continued running up a short embankment and stopped at the edge of the road.

"Daddy, that's your truck."

"Well, so it is. Come here."

The pickup bed was covered with a heavy canvas tarp. He opened the tailgate and released one end of the rope so part of the tarp slowly fell into the bed. He picked up Roberta and sat her on the edge of the tailgate.

"What, Daddy? What?"

"Well, I was over talking with Grandpa Newsom, and he had a problem."

"What was the problem?"

"He needs some help, and he's wondering if you would be able to help him?"

"What can I do?"

"Well, you see, he knew that I was going away, and that there would be more space in the house without me there."

"Does Grandpa Newsom want to move to our house?"

"No, no. But he was hoping you'd be able to take care of …"

He flipped up the end of the tarp to reveal a metal cage. He flipped the latch and out charged a small dog, a terrier, wagging and barking, and immediately ran into Roberta's arms.

"You remember Trigger, right?"

Roberta laughed and smiled as the dog acquainted itself with every square inch of her face as if it was a plate of beef gravy.

"Trigger!"

"Do you think you'd be able to take care of Trigger for Grandpa Newsom?"

"Do you mean it?"

"Yes, just until I get back. Could you?"

"Yes, Daddy. Yes!"

Joy covered the moment, pushing back the anxiety and the tears. She would have a dog. One to care for. One to use Daddy's space until he returned.

"Now Grandpa Newsom loves this dog."

"So do I, Daddy."

"You gotta remember to walk him and feed him and …"

"Thank you, Daddy."

Her mother appeared from the road side of the truck and squeezed in next to her husband. He put his arm around her, and she tucked her head onto his shoulder as they both watched Roberta smother her new dog.

Roberta caught a glimpse of something flying. White. And it flitted in the air and landed on her father's shoulder.

"Look, Daddy. A butterfly."

He turned his head, slid his finger under the insect, and lifted it towards Roberta.

"It's a moth."

"A moth?"

"Yes, but it flies like a butterfly."

"Mommy, I found a caterpillar and named it Mommy."

"Oh, you did?" she chuckled.

The moth took off. Roberta slid off the tailgate and motioned for Trigger to follow her. He didn't hesitate.

"Let's chase the moth, Trigger."

The moth zigzagged around several trees, and the two new best friends traipsed after it, with laughs and barks, and a camaraderie forged through instant trust and respect. Her mother and father followed her, hand in hand, as the moth led them to the lake. Roberta stood at the edge of the lake, Trigger paw deep in the gentle laps of the water.

"Fly moth. Fly. Go across the lake. Go moth. Fly."

Her parents came in behind her.

"Roberta, do you still see it?"

"It's there Daddy. Tiny white dot. It's still moving."

The dot disappeared into the ashen sky and became one with the backdrop of the lake.

"I can't see it anymore. Come back and visit me, moth." Roberta stared across the lake and saw the distant tree tops from the other side. She remembered what her father had told her. "Daddy?"

"Yes, sweetheart."

"Will you come back from the lake?"

He knelt down and squared her shoulders with his face. "Nothing will keep me away from you. Nothing."

They hugged as her mother rubbed her husband's shoulder with one hand and wiped a tear with another.

Chapter 3

Christmas in '44

Jolting. Christmas Eve flooded Roberta's mind with hurried images of people and emotions and things that didn't matter. Her mother fed her a steady stream of gingerbread boys, as many as she wanted, and she nibbled on them in the midst of confusion. On the stairs. Under the tree. On the sofa. In the kitchen. In her bedroom. Everywhere she went, she carried a half-eaten gingerbread boy, and Trigger, of course, was never more than a step behind, ready to comfort her.

The Dwyers came but didn't stay. Their children looked shell-shocked. They stared at Roberta but didn't speak. Mrs. Dwyer hugged Roberta's mother more than once and kept repeating the phrase: "… if there's anything we can do."

Roberta looked at Robbie Dwyer, her same age, and then at Mr. Dwyer. She had a question. A burning one she had to ask Robbie's father.

"Are you going across the lake?"

Everyone looked at her. Her mother explained what she meant, and Mr. Dwyer gave an answer Roberta didn't understand. He spoke about his knee for some reason. Little Robbie Dwyer just stared at her without saying a word until his mother prodded him to be polite. "Merry Christmas," he said, without a hint of irony. It would be a merry one for him. Isn't Christmas always merry, regardless? Roberta latched on to the phrase and repeated it in her mind: *Merry Christmas. Merry Christmas.* As the family left, she yelled it audibly: "Merry Christmas." Then took a bite of her gingerbread boy.

Grandma Newsom arrived just as the Dwyers were leaving. Grandma greeted her with a hug and gave her a bag full of penny candy. Peppermints, mainly. Grandpa Newsom used to give her peppermints in church every Sunday. It seemed the equivalent of keeping a dog from barking by feeding it steak, but Roberta didn't mind. She loved them, and now she had a bag full of peppermints and an army of gingerbread boys, who followed her around the house aimlessly.

A Christmas drama was being broadcast on the radio. Grandma kept trying to get Roberta to listen, but the girl couldn't stay still, and mainly watched her mother. Every time her mother went into the kitchen, Roberta could hear the crying.

Her grandma would go in and comfort her but would be back in a minute or two to see if Roberta needed anything. She had her sweets and her dog. What else was there?

Pastor Jenkins and his wife stopped over as well. They gave them two loaves of bread and a fruitcake. As the evening wore on, those two loaves would multiply into many more, not unlike the miracle of Jesus, as neighbors and friends dropped off an endless supply of baked goods for the family as an offering of condolence.

The pastor made a point to speak to Roberta, but she had trouble concentrating. She did ask one question.

"Pastor Jenkins, where do people go when they don't return from the lake?"

Her mother explained the meaning, and Pastor Jenkins knelt down in front of the girl and told her plainly. "Heaven, my child. Your father was a good man. He is happy in heaven. It's very sad for us here on earth, but your father is not sad. Not today."

That thought rested uneasily on Roberta. *Why wouldn't he be sad if he wasn't with his family? Why would he be happy to be away from us? Forever?* The great disconnect confused her mind, and she refused to smile for the rest of the pastor's visit. The pastor prayed for their family before he left.

Everyone sat in the living room, head down, dreariness dripping from every part of their bodies, and they listened to the words. Roberta opened her eyes and peeked through the cracks between her fingers. The pastor's wife held a handkerchief over her face. The pastor clenched his hands together with interlocking fingers and prayed with a sincere intensity. Her mother sat behind Roberta, holding hands with her grandmother. There were not many words that Roberta comprehended, but she grasped onto a few: hope, peace, heaven.

Shortly after they left, Roberta's mother took her to her bedroom. She didn't say anything. She laid down beside her and Roberta drifted off to sleep, exhausted in thoughts. She woke once in the middle of the night to see her mother curled up beside her sleeping, but when she woke in the morning, only Trigger remained. She wrapped herself in a warm housecoat and plodded down the steps one at a time, still wiping the night from her eyes. The living room was dark, but the morning light had begun to illuminate the room through the window. She opened the front door and allowed Trigger to run out into the morning. She heard something in the kitchen. Grandma. Warming milk on the stove.

"Hot chocolate?"

"Yes, please."

"Where's Mom?"

"She's still sleeping. She needs to rest."

Grandma Newsom stepped towards Roberta and gave her a hug.

"It's Christmas morning."

"Uh-huh. Merry Christmas, Grandma."

"Yes." She seemed to shrug the thought off. "I'll tell you what. Why don't you go look under the tree and see what Santa Claus brought you."

"I don't believe in Santa Claus."

"Well, all right. Why don't you go see? I'll bring your hot chocolate."

Roberta heard Trigger scratching at the door and let him in. She turned on the lamp next to the sofa and sat on the floor near the tree. Trigger jumped into her lap.

"Your paws are wet." She didn't bother pushing him away.

Several neatly wrapped presents sat under the tree. The anticipation of their contents was tempered by the silent cloud hanging over the house. Roberta touched a couple of the gifts gently but left them alone. She stood up and climbed into the sofa knee-first, putting her arms on the back of the cushions, and stared out the picture window, across the street to the lake in the distance. The white ground extended far out into the lake like a sheet of paper. She thought of that day by the lake with her father and the moth, wondering if the moth ever made it across and what had become of the caterpillar.

"Roberta, your hot chocolate is ready."

"Could I have some too?" Her mother stood halfway up the stairs, wrapped in a wool housecoat, and smiled at her daughter. Roberta jumped off the sofa, and they hugged each other at the bottom of the stairs.

They congregated around the tree with piping hot mugs as Roberta opened her first gift. A new dress from her grandmother. It was yellow, her favorite color. She thought of wearing it to church. She always wore a dress to church. She thought of seeing Grandpa Newsom at the funeral home, lying unresponsive. His eyes closed. Bouquets of flowers sprouting up around his casket as if he laid in a bed of flowers. All colors. Even yellow ones. She remembered wearing a dress that day, but it was black.

"Did Grandpa Newsom like flowers?"

Grandma had a strange look on her face. "Yes, he always helped me plant the annuals in the flower bed each spring. Why do you ask?"

"I remember the flowers at his funeral. Many of them were yellow."

Her mother glanced over at Grandma and

smiled. She patted Roberta on the back.

"Mom, why did I wear a black dress to Grandpa's funeral?"

Her mother hesitated. "Black is the color of mourning."

"Morning? I thought the sky was red in the morning."

"No. Mourning means when someone has died and you feel bad and think about your memories with that person. So we dress in black to show that we are sad."

"If someone is going to heaven like Pastor Jenkins said, and they are going to be happy in heaven, shouldn't we wear a bright color? Like this." She held up her new dress. "Could I wear this to father's funeral?"

Her mother put her hand to her face and quietly whispered, "Excuse me." She ran up the stairs to the second floor.

"Mom?"

"Roberta, give your mother a moment."

"Did I say something wrong?"

"No, no. Not at all. Why don't you open this gift?"

"We should wait for mom."

"No, go ahead. She won't mind."

She unfastened the tape on the edge of the package covered with green wrapping paper with decorated Christmas trees on it. In a paper box was a doll. In a dress. She had pigtails and black buckled shoes. Roberta held it in her lap.

"Such a beautiful doll," said her grandmother. "Do you like her?"

Roberta nodded but didn't say anything. She rubbed the doll's head then lifted it up for Trigger to see. He raised his head but didn't move from repose behind Roberta's back.

"And you also have your stocking. Here. I think you'll find some treats in there."

"Thank you, Grandma."

Her grandma handed her a long red stocking filled with fruit and tightly wrapped confectionery. Roberta removed a peppermint stick from the stocking and placed it in her hot chocolate.

"Do you want one, Grandma?"

"No, thank you."

"Roberta?" Her mother called from the stairs. She carried a gift the size of a shoe box. Roberta didn't stand up, but watched as her mother placed it in front of her.

"There's one more gift. This is from your father." She was holding back tears when she said it. "Open it, Roberta."

"From Daddy?"

"Yes. He asked me to order it for you because

he couldn't be here."

The sheer weight of that statement rested heavily on everyone in the room. He couldn't be there, and he never would be again. The last gift she would ever get from her father.

"This was specially for you. Open it."

She did. A wooden model airplane. Bi-wings. Painted on each side were angels and on the tail were the words: Angel Wings.

Her eyes lit. "An airplane." It's what she wanted. She stood to her feet and allowed the wings to catch the draft. It soared like her soul, and she sped around the house in a moment of play with Trigger following her with a playful bark. Both Grandma and Mother had moved to the sofa, each with smiles on their faces.

"This is the best gift ever."

She continued making another loop. Living room. Dining room. Kitchen. Then back.

"And we're going to go across the lake. We're going to fly and soar into the sky. And we'll find daddy across the lake. And—"

Roberta kept talking like that, about what she wanted to do. Her mother tried to intervene and stop her from speaking so unrealistically. But Grandma Newsom told her to let it go.

"Let the girl play and have a moment."

Roberta heard her but didn't stop. Her mind

climbed into the clouds. She could see the lake far below her and then the shore. The far shore. It was within reach. As the plane descended for a landing, she knew that she was closer to her father wherever he was. She was closer. Maybe to heaven. Maybe to the funeral home. Maybe to the carved stone in the cemetery. Wherever she was, she was happier with an airplane in her hands.

Chapter 4

The Hard Ground

On the day after Christmas, Roberta had one activity in mind. Flying. Grandma Newsom was still at the house and greeted her with fresh pancakes that the girl couldn't refuse. Every pilot needs their fuel. Her mother wasn't around yet. After breakfast, Roberta emerged into the snowy morning bundled from head to toe in nearly every piece of warm clothing she had. Knit cap on her head. Scarf around her neck. New Christmas mittens which held her precious Angel Wings airplane.

"Come on, Trigger."

The pair crossed the road—not yet plowed— and the muted sound of the fresh-morning snow made her voice and Trigger's bark feel distant. She held the wooden plane high above her head and used her lips to rumble out the sound of the engine. The snow buried her feet to her ankles with every step, and the heavy wet flakes added to the pileup with each passing minute.

She wanted to try it. The ice on the lake. Just once. She knew she wasn't allowed, but the plane wanted to keep soaring. It wanted to glide across the open wind of the water, much like the moth once did. Roberta repressed her mother's warning about the lake and had a few thoughts of her own: *It's ice. Very thick. I'll just take one step and see how it feels. It looks strong.*

She stepped out off the snowy edge onto the ice. It felt hard yet slick.

"Look, Trigger. I'm standing on the water. The plane is flying. It wants to soar, but I have to be careful with it. Have to make sure the ice is safe."

She took another step and turned around when she heard Trigger bark at something behind them.

"What do you see, boy?"

Then she saw it too. Mr. Goodwin's truck. He had the only truck in the neighborhood with a large snow blade, and he proudly sloshed through the streets after every snow like an army general in a tank. The truck puttered towards Roberta's house. Trigger barked incessantly and had run half the fifty yards back to the road.

"Trigger. Come back."

Mr. Goodwin's blade had gotten caught on something a couple houses before Roberta's. He emerged from the cab and inspected the front end. Satisfied, he climbed back into the truck, reversed a few feet, then continued his plowing.

Trigger had made his way to the edge of the road, and Roberta kept calling to him. That's when Roberta saw her mother on the front porch of her house, waving her hands. She yelled something, but Roberta couldn't hear. She yelled again, and Trigger bolted across the street.

"No, Trigger!"

Mr. Goodwin hit the brakes, but the ice underneath locked the truck's wheels in a forward slide. The blade hit Trigger with full force and pushed him towards the snow bank. The truck careened to its side and wedged Trigger between the edge of the blade and the cement slab of the Ares' family sidewalk. The dog lay yelping on the side of the street. Mrs. Ares ran towards it, wearing only her housecoat and slippers. Mr. Goodwin raised the snow blade, which released the pressure on the dog. Roberta, who had watched the entire incident from the edge of the lake, sprinted towards her dog, yelling its name after each plodding step in the half-foot deep snow. Mr. Goodwin had straightened out the truck and pulled it up in front of the sidewalk before he opened the cab door and stepped out. As he reached the dog, Roberta had arrived at the street, and she called for both her mom and the dog.

Trigger lay mostly silent. He lifted his head

once when he heard Roberta's voice but then laid it back in the snow. His side had a deep cut and blood seeped into the snow turning it dark red.

"Trigger!"

"I'm so sorry, Mrs. Ares. I tried to stop but—"

"It's not your fault, Mr. Goodwin. The poor dog ran right in front of you."

"Mom, do something. We have to help him."

"Mr. Goodwin, is there anything we can do?"

"Look at the poor thing. He's in pain. He's barely responsive."

"Mom! Trigger!"

"Roberta, calm."

"Mom, we have to do something!"

"He's hurting, Roberta."

"Mrs. Ares, I'm afraid he needs to be put down. There's nothing we can do."

"Put down?" asked Roberta. "What does that mean?"

"Roberta—"

"Mom, do something."

"Roberta, there's nothing we can do. I'm sorry."

"Mom? What do you mean? We have to stop the bleeding."

"We can't, Roberta. Trigger is in pain. We need to take away his pain. And there's only one way to do that."

"Mrs. Ares, I have my hunting rifle in the cab. Take the child inside. Let me take care of it."

Hunting rifle. The words made no sense to Roberta. Of what use was a hunting rifle? There was nothing to hunt here. They needed a doctor, someone who could help and make Trigger better. Of what use was a rifle?

Roberta's mom put her arm around her child. "I'm sorry, Roberta, but Trigger is going to die. There's nothing we can do. I'm so sorry."

Die. Dead. The same word reverberated through her head once again.

"No!" She sobbed and leaned down to Trigger's ear. "It's all right, boy. Roberta's here. I'm going to take care of you. It's alright boy." She had removed her mittens and was rubbing his head. The dog's eyes were closed and its breathing was shallow but still visible.

"Roberta …"

Her mother kept talking to her, but she didn't listen. She remained focused on her dog and whispered sweet words. "Remember, Daddy said you could stay here while he's gone. Don't worry, boy. Don't worry."

She heard the cab door of the truck open.

"I'll take good care of you."

Then it slammed shut, and Mr. Goodwin's footsteps sloshed towards them.

"Trigger. Good boy, good boy."

"Roberta."

"I'm right here, Trigger. I'm right here."

"Roberta, I'm sorry, but you have to let him go."

She was ready to say something, but she felt a shadow over top of her. Like an ominous mountain rose behind her, and she looked up to see Mr. Goodwin holding a rifle across his chest.

"What are you going to do? Mom?"

"Roberta. Come with me," said her mother.

"Mom, no. What is he going to do?"

"I'm sorry, Roberta," said Mr. Goodwin.

"Roberta, Trigger is gone. We need to take his pain away. I'm so sorry."

Her mother reached down and grabbed Roberta from behind and embraced her. She pulled Roberta to her feet, convulsing and crying. She yelled and screamed both the dog's name and for her mother. She couldn't understand why. She didn't want to understand why. All she knew was that a cruel man stood over her dog with a rifle, and her mother allowed it and even encouraged it.

"Roberta, let's go into the house."

"No."

"Roberta."

She glanced up to the house and Grandma

Newsom stood on the front porch, hand over her mouth. *It was her dog, once. She'd understand.*

"Grandma! Grandma!"

"Listen to your mother, Roberta. I'm so sorry."

"Mom!"

"Let's go in the house."

"No, no. I'm not leaving him. I'm not leaving."

Her mother pulled her back away from the sidewalk and nodded to Mr. Goodwin. Roberta could see him out of the corner of his eye. He positioned himself between her and the dog. She noticed his shoulders rise, and then an echoed thunderclap pierced the dull morning. It jerked her and everyone. The whimpering was over, but the crying had just began.

"Trigger!"

"I'm sorry, Roberta. I'm so sorry."

"Trigger!"

She tried to break free, but her mother held her tightly.

"Trigger's gone, Roberta. I'm so sorry. Shhhh."

She pulled Roberta to her chest. Snow continued to fall. Grandma Newsom held her hand over her mouth. Roberta's mom wept, as did her daughter. The deafening silence of the snow was only broken by the footsteps of Mr. Goodwin, who had retrieved a burlap sack from the cab of the truck and placed the remains inside.

"Mrs. Ares, would you like me to dispose of this?"

Dispose. Dead. The words rattled again in Roberta's mind. Her mother had let go of her, and she saw the weight of the sack in Mr. Goodwin's hands. Her dog was in a bag. The bag was tied shut. The dog would never leave the bag again. Drops of blood seeped through the lowest point of the bag. The drops added to the blood red color already present in the snow. Roberta approached Mr. Goodwin and stared him in the face, but she didn't say anything. The look in her eyes said everything. Mr. Goodwin talked, apologies, words of sympathy, telling her that the dog was in a better place, it was at peace, no longer suffering. In the midst of all the explanations, Roberta said one thing.

"Dead."

"Yes, Roberta," said her mother.

"Trigger is dead."

"Yes, Roberta."

"Where will we bury him?" Her demeanor had settled into an emotionless state. She had something on her mind and would be satisfied. "Where will you bury him?"

"I'll take care of it, Roberta. You don't have to worry about it."

"Where?"

"I'll see to it that he has a proper burial."

"Where?"

"I—"

His words were vacant of meaning, and she remained unsatisfied. She wanted more, and her mother spoke up.

"Roberta, where would you like to bury Trigger?"

"Beside Grandpa Newsom, in the cemetery. He loved the dog too."

"We can't do that," she replied.

"Why not?"

"The cemetery is only for people, Roberta. They won't accept dogs."

Mr. Goodwin had placed the sack into the back of the pick-up. "But don't worry," he said. "I'll take good care of it."

"Mom, don't let him take Trigger. Don't let him."

"Roberta, he's helping us out, and he'll find a good spot to—"

"Don't let him! I promised Daddy that Trigger would be here until he gets home. He can't leave. He can't. We have to bury him here. Mom!"

Roberta spoke the words, in a near scream, into the air—her entire body tense and throbbing.

"Could we, Mr. Goodwin? Do you think we

could bury the dog in the backyard?"

He shook his head in doubt. "I don't know. The ground's awfully frozen. It's been cold now for three weeks. It won't be easy to dig a hole."

"Mom, I want him buried in the backyard. Mom!"

She turned back to him. "Is there anyway?"

He hesitated. "Well, I suppose I could start a fire. That should soften up the dirt enough, if you want. It's going to take some time, and I won't be able to do it until later today."

"Thank you, Mr. Goodwin."

Roberta thought it strange that her mother was thanking the man who hit her dog with the truck and shot her dog with a rifle. Something cruel hung in the whole exchange, as if right behavior changed places with wrong behavior. As if being a human was not just about following the Golden Rule like they emphasized in Sunday School. She had no intention of ever shooting Mr. Goodwin's dog. There was something deeper and darker than a nine-year-old could fully understand. But she felt it, clearly, in her chest, and she wondered when it would make sense, if ever.

Chapter 5

The Fire

Each hour passed like a slow cog churning memories in Roberta's mind. Her mother took her in the house and tried to convince her of many things. "It's not anyone's fault. It was an accident. A terrible accident. Cry. Let yourself cry. Trigger isn't in pain anymore." The words did little to brighten her mood. Her grandmother baked her a cake and served it mid-morning. She ate it. It tasted good yet left her feeling unsure. The sweetness teased her senses as if a cake could substitute itself for the hole left in her heart. Two holes in less than two full days.

The sack, dripping red droplets into the snow, remained a constant image in her mind. From the living room window, she watched her grandmother take a bucket of hot water to the sidewalk and pour it over the red snow, melting the color into the hard crusted soil.

How would she remember Trigger?

"Mom, do we have a photo of Trigger?"

She didn't. "I have one at home," said Grandma Newsom. "It's of your grandpa and

Trigger sitting together on our front porch. Your father took it for us. I'll bring it over. You can have it. Would you like that?"

She nodded. But the sack remained full. The dog had been shot. The pellets of the shotgun cartridge had ripped life-ending paths through Trigger. Then Mr. Goodwin placed the body in a sack like husks of corn or rotten cabbages. She remembered how daddy would place the leftover food in a sack like that and give it to Farmer Johns for his pigs. But a sack with a dog had to go in the ground.

Another thought.

"Mom?"

They sat at the kitchen table after lunch. They had eaten tomato soup. No one was particularly hungry after the mid-morning cake.

"Yes, Roberta."

"When Grandpa died, he didn't have a sack."

"Oh …"

Grandma Newsom patted Roberta's hand and nodded to her daughter Tricia as if telling her that she would answer this one.

"Roberta, when a person dies, they are put in a coffin made out of wood."

Roberta thought for a moment. "Then why was Trigger put in a sack? Why doesn't he have a coffin?"

Each adult looked uncomfortable. How to answer such a question to a girl who feels love, perhaps an indistinguishable love, between her father who was dead and her dog who was shot and put in a sack?

"Roberta," Grandma continued. Mother held back tears with her elbows on the table and her hands covering her face up to her eyes. "Animals are different than humans."

"But didn't we love Trigger, like we loved Daddy?"

"Excuse me." Her mother stood and left the room. Roberta had witnessed her retreat many times since Christmas Eve.

"Mom misses Daddy. I miss Trigger. Daddy gave me Trigger."

"Poor child." Grandma patted the child's hands with care. "Roberta, let me tell you a story. Before you were born, your grandpa and I had another dog. Ginger."

"Ginger?"

"She was crippled in her legs."

"What does that mean?"

"Her front legs bent in like this." She turned in her elbow to demonstrate the crooked, inward turn of Ginger's legs. "But that never slowed her down. She was an outdoor dog. Stayed in a pen out back. When we were in the yard, she'd run around with all the kids, including your mother. And Aunt Laura."

"What happened to Ginger?"

"It was a cold winter night. We had given Ginger blankets and straw in her little house we built her, but that morning Grandpa Newsom went out to feed Ginger and she had died. Grandpa Newsom felt really bad that she died in the cold. He was upset at himself. Said he should have brought Ginger in the house."

Roberta's face look worried. She imagined a limp dog on the white snow, unresponsive, just like Trigger.

"Ginger was 13 years old. She had lived a long and good life. But Grandpa Newsom always felt bad about that incident, and you know what? When we got Trigger many years later, Grandpa Newsom always kept him in the house. I think he did it as a way to remember Ginger."

Roberta dipped another cracker into the soup but just played with it.

"It's always difficult losing a dog. They become part of the family. Accidents happen. Bad things happen in this world. Sometimes they're out of our control. Trigger didn't do anything wrong when he crossed the road. Mr. Goodwin didn't do anything wrong when he was plowing snow. It's no one's fault; all we can do is to remember why we loved Trigger. Just like your grandpa and I always remembered Ginger. Think of the good memories of playing together." Grandma stopped speaking. A silent moment passed. "Do you want another piece of cake?"

Roberta nodded. "Grandma, did Ginger have a sack like Trigger."

Her Grandma paused for a moment. "You know, Sweetheart, I can't remember what your grandpa did with Ginger. But I know he gave her the respect she deserved. And he showed that respect to Trigger when he got him. If your grandpa was here when it happened, he would have helped you do the right thing for Trigger, because he knows what you're feeling."

Her grandmother went to the counter and sliced another piece of cake.

"Grandma, was daddy's death an accident?"

"Your daddy was a hero. That's all you need to know."

"Grandma, so Mr. Goodwin didn't do anything wrong when he shot Trigger?"

Grandma sighed. "No. Life is complicated. Sometimes the kindest thing to do is to allow someone to leave. It was Trigger's time to go, and Mr. Goodwin helped us."

"It doesn't seem nice."

"I know, Roberta. It doesn't."

***

Around 4:30 PM, the dim gray winter sky faded as the long night descended on the Ares family. Mr. Goodwin had just arrived. He parked his truck in the driveway and met Mrs. Ares on the back porch for a brief conversation. Roberta watched from the window of her second story bedroom overlooking the backyard. Mr. Goodwin trudged through the snow and chose a patch of ground near the field in the background, in front of the row of bushes, and behind the swing set. He used a snow shovel to clear out a patch. He confirmed the firmness of the ground with a regular shovel, and then carried handfuls of firewood from the truck and stacked it at the chosen location. He arranged the wood in a tee-pee configuration, poured a liquid over it, and lit a match. He backed away and tossed the match towards the wood. It went out. He tried a second match and this time fire exploded to the height of Mr. Goodwin himself and engulfed the wood. He backed away and watched the fire take hold. He added additional wood to the pile and prodded it with a shovel until it roared steadily, a vibrant orange glow against the darkening backdrop of the approaching night.

The fire mesmerized Roberta. She held the airplane in her hand and wondered about the location of the sack. Probably the back of the truck. *Would there still be blood dripping? Was Trigger just lying in the back of the truck all day? All alone? In the cold? Just like Ginger? But if he's dead, does it matter?* She entertained every question in her mind until her mother's voice interrupted her.

"You see that Mr. Goodwin is here?"

"Ah-huh."

"Do you want me to watch with you?"

She nodded, and her mother sat with her daughter on the small bench under the window, the same place her parents would sometimes read to her.

"Mom, how long will the fire burn?"

"Mr. Goodwin said a couple hours. He'll leave and come back."

"Can I go out to the fire?"

"Roberta, I don't think you should—"

"Please, Mom."

"Wait till he leaves, and then we'll go out together for a short time. All right?"

After thirty minutes of tending the fire, Mr. Goodwin left, telling Mrs. Ares that he'd be back in the evening to bury Trigger.

"Do you want to go out now?" she called to Roberta.

"In a minute."

Roberta sat at a small table in her room with a paper and a charcoal pencil in her hand. She drew four legs and a small head with pointed ears. She drew an eyeball and a curved line for a smile. Across the top she spelled out the name: T-R-I-G-G-E-R. Underneath the dog she wrote: G-O-O-D-B-Y-E. She carried it to the bottom of the steps, put on her coat, and walked through the kitchen. Her mother, already bundled up, grabbed the long metal tube flashlight with a wide round reflector on the end, almost as large as a car headlamp.

"What do you have there, Roberta?"

She showed her mother the picture, with Grandma looking on, and they exited the house into the dark. The snow crunched under their feet as they traced the path that Mr. Goodwin had used to carry to the wood. The fire burned vibrantly and they stood around its glow in silent homage to its meaning.

"Goodbye, Trigger. I love you."

She placed the drawing on the periphery of the fire, and it lit around its edges, burning inward over the words until the dog's image had been engulfed in the flames. Neither spoke in the solemn moment. The fire's light flickered in the shadows of the rim of snow. Roberta stared deep into the light. She thought how the ashes would give way to a hole where the sack would be buried.

"Mom, how did Daddy die?"

"Roberta, he died a hero."

"But how?"

"Roberta, don't think about that. Think about how much he loved you."

"He promised he would come back."

"Oh, Roberta."

She put her arm around her and tugged her inward against her coat.

"Daddy was in the war."

"That's right."

"They shoot each other in war."

"Roberta, war is not something a nine-year-old should worry about. It's a terrible thing. It's cruel and mean, but sometimes people fight. They have to."

"And they shoot at each other? Just like Mr. Goodwin. He had to shoot Trigger?"

Tricia paused and released an audible sigh. "That wasn't war, Roberta, but yes. Sometimes we have to shoot."

"Did someone shoot daddy?"

"Oh, Roberta. No, honey. No. Your daddy died in an airplane crash." The cold froze the droplets from Tricia's eyes. "Come, Roberta. Let's go inside. It's getting too cold."

"One more minute."

"All right."

***

Around seven-thirty, Roberta heard a truck pull into the driveway. Mr. Goodwin had returned. She ran upstairs to her room to have a full view of the yard. Mr. Goodwin carried two lit lanterns up the snowy path to the patch of ground which smoldered with specks of light. He placed the lanterns on both sides of the fire and picked up a shovel and dug around a few times. He scraped the smoldering wood to the side and tested the dirt. He dug several times and threw the dirt over top of the embers of the wood. He continued digging. Roberta watched each heave of the shovel until he stopped, placed the shovel on the ground, picked up a lantern, and walked back down the path. She couldn't see the back of the truck, but he emerged into sight once again carrying the sack in his right arm. He placed the sack in the hole and without any hesitation, started pitching the dirt back into the hole.

"Mom! Mom!"

Her mother ran upstairs and frantically asked what was the matter.

"He's burying Trigger. He's throwing dirt on the pile. He's burying Trigger."

Her mother said nothing, and they watched the flickering light from the lanterns as he patted the dirt with the back of the shovel.

"Roberta, he's coming to the house. I have to go down."

Roberta followed, and they held the storm door open with the main door shut behind them.

"Mrs. Ares. It's finished."

"Thank you, Mr. Goodwin."

Roberta still had a hard time hearing thanks coming from her mother.

"Roberta," he looked at her. She had tucked herself behind her mother with only her head peering out from the side. "I'm very sorry for your loss. Both of them. I wish my truck could have stopped in time. I surely do."

"It's not your fault, Mr. Goodwin," said her mother. "We appreciate all you did for us today."

"Let me know if there's anything else I can do, not that ..."

He looked awkward and didn't finish his thought.

"Thank you."

"Again. Very sorry about your dog."

Roberta had one unsettled thought in her mind. It burst from her without effort. "What about the stone?" Her mother looked down at her. "The stone. Where's Trigger's stone?"

"What stone?"

"Like Grandpa Newsom. When we go to the cemetery, he has a stone with his name carved in it. Where's Trigger's stone?"

"Roberta— "

"He has to have a stone. How else could I visit him? How else will I know where he is? How else will I remember him?"

"Roberta, we don't have a stone for Trigger."

"Will you get one?"

"Well, I don't know. We can't do it now, Roberta."

"Why? Why not?" The tears were forming and her words cried out as harsh as the biting wind.

"Roberta."

"Mom, he has to have a stone."

She was weeping. Fully. Loud deep breathes exhaled like stuttering coughs. She kept calling for a stone again and again. Her distraught mother looked at the unsure-of-himself Mr. Goodwin. She didn't know what to do. She looked at him for help. Anything that might relieve a little of the pain.

"Ma'am, why don't I put a pole in the ground tonight? That way you'll know exactly where the dog was buried. Then you can decide later on, when the weather improves, what you want to do to commemorate the dog."

"Thank you, Mr. Goodwin. Thank you. Roberta, you hear that? We'll put a pole there for now, and then we'll figure it out. We'll get the stone, all right? When the weather gets better, we'll find a good way to mark Trigger's grave so you can always remember. All right? I promise."

Roberta affirmed through the sobbing. Mr. Goodwin walked back to the truck and put a wooden pole two feet into the ground. The three watched from the window inside the house. They could only see the flickering of the lantern, until even that faded out of sight and they heard the rumble of the truck back down the driveway and disappear into the darkness.

Chapter 6

The Service

Pastor Jenkins visited the Ares' house several times during the week after the devastating news of Mr. Ares' death. Others visited as well, and Roberta had to watch her mother regularly excuse herself from the room. Grandma Newsom would step in to offer the guest a muffin or cake to mitigate the awkward situation.

Difficult conversations became commonplace. The discussion concerning the memorial service being the hardest.

"Roberta, Pastor Jenkins is going to organize a community memorial service for your daddy on New Year's Eve. This Sunday."

"What's a memorial service?"

"Remember when Grandpa Newsom died? We all went to the funeral home and people talked about what a wonderful person he was? That's what's going to happen at the church for your father."

"Why at the church?"

"It's a convenient place for everyone from the

community to meet?"

"What about his body?"

"What?"

"Daddy's body? Will it be in a coffin like Grandpa Newsom?"

Her mother flinched in emotion but held it straight. "No, Roberta. There is no coffin."

"Why not?"

"There just isn't."

"What happened to Daddy's body?"

"He was buried over there."

"Across the lake?"

"Yes, across the lake."

She thought for a moment. "But Mom, Daddy said he would come back. Why don't they bring his body back? Why can't we bury it beside Trigger then I can visit both of them?"

"Oh, Roberta." She hugged her daughter and didn't respond to anymore of her questions.

***

It seemed as if the entire town showed up at the Methodist church to show respect for the fallen. It was not the first community service for a dead soldier. They had become a normal part of the local fabric, but they were never mundane. Never cursory. Each one hurt just as much, and sometimes more than the last.

Roberta, her mother, and her grandmother walked the center aisle towards the front. They all wore black dresses. Roberta did not like hers at all. She scoffed at its drabness, and knew that daddy would have liked her yellow Christmas dress. But her mother wouldn't listen and forced her to wear the black costume. It was the antipathy of a bridal processional—the flower girl without flowers—the bride without a groom. Congregates flooded the side aisles with stupefied and unsmiling faces from all walks of life, watching the three pass by aisle after aisle. Some nodded. Others cried. Most just gawked. It wasn't clear what they looked for. Reaction. Spectacle. A feeling of hopelessness, wondering internally if they would be as stoic and regal as the three steel-faced mourners. Little did the onlookers know that the Ares' family cache of tears had been extinguished. But not for long. Never for long.

Pastor Jenkins clung to the sides of the pulpit in a solemn stare. The left front row had been reserved for the three, and they sat alone, a buffer of space to their left and right to further signify the difference between them and the rest. Roberta sat between the two matriarchs of the family. Her eyes trained on the pastor who began speaking and asked one and all to lower their heads in prayer. As he spoke about God's work and God's healing, Roberta looked behind her. Each row like the other—heads tilted earthward. A sea of conformity except for one pair of eyes belonging to a boy three rows back on the opposite side— Robbie Dwyer. He had placed his hand in front of his mouth and nose but did little to hide the fact that he freely looked around the sanctuary. Their eyes locked together. He didn't flinch, and neither did Roberta. She noticed his father sitting next to him and wondered why it felt so unfair. She thought how when the prayer ended, all eyes would be back on her. No one would notice Robbie at the end of the prayer, but everyone would stare at the girl in the black dress. It was like she wore a target on her back and the daggers dug into her skin regardless of whether they were looking. She wanted to be like Robbie. Invisible. Just a child. But she was more than that, and though she couldn't understand exactly what she was, she knew that people would never look at her the same way again.

"She's the girl who lost her father."

"Poor child."

Her position in the pew had secured her future.

Roberta turned away from Robbie's stare, and

as the pastor's invocation ended, she leaned over to her mother.

"Mom, where's the coffin?"

"Shhh. Roberta, we talked about this. There isn't a coffin."

Roberta turned back to the pastor. Bouquets of flowers surrounded the pulpit and lined the entire edge of the platform on both sides. Roberta wondered why there were flowers. Beautiful flowers in the dead of winter. Where did they get them? Why was the pulpit allowed to be beautiful with color when she had to wear a drab black dress?

The words from the front faded in and out of her consciousness.

"… and anyone who would like to say a few words can come to the front in a moment …"

Would I be allowed, she thought. If she wanted to speak. What would she say to the group of eyes?

"… to honor Major Daniel Antonios Ares, beloved husband, father, community member …"

Daniel caught her ear. Daniel. It's a name she knew. Her father's name. But it felt distant, like the expanse of the lake, like a familiar faded memory. Daniel. Daddy. That's what came to her mind. Daniel. Daddy. His face seemed blurred in her memory. She thought of his smile. He always smiled around her. He would pick her up and hold her on his shoulder. He would tickle her under the covers, and lay down on her bed, and they would look at the ceiling and the shadows from the night light, and he would sing a song or two and she would go to sleep and wake in the morning to eggs, pancakes, and Daddy. And he would walk her to the school bus and pat her on the back.

"… the God we know in blessing is the same God we know in grief …"

Blessing. Grief. All the words confused her. And where was the coffin? *Grandma Newsom said that Grandpa had a coffin. Everyone who dies has a coffin. Except Trigger. He has a sack and a hole in the ground.*

Thoughts tripped over thoughts, and she wondered why she had to sit there. *Why did they leave the body over there, across the lake?* It didn't make sense to her.

"Mom? The coffin."

"Shhhh."

"… this tragic loss …"

She stood up. Even though she was small, everyone in the church still had a view of her. Her mother tugged at her sleeve, trying to pull her back into the seat, but she struggled and pulled away. The pastor stumbled over a few of his words as his attention had been drawn to her. She walked a few steps towards the center aisle.

"Where's the coffin?" It was a pleading sound, that of an earnest bird chirping for a morning breakfast, anticipating a mother's return to the nest. Confident that it would happen. "If someone dies, there must be a coffin. Grandma said so."

The entire congregation froze. All eyes trained on her just as she imagined they were anyways. What was the difference? But she didn't think of them at all. Only the body that was missing.

"Where's Daddy? He said he was coming home. I don't believe it." She shouted. "I don't believe it. Where's the coffin? Where's the body? He's across the lake, and he'll return. He promised."

Her mother tried to stand and stop the clamoring child, but she didn't. Nor did she run out of the room as she normally would. She just lowered her head and cried. Grandma Newsom patted Tricia's arm and stood up and put her arm around Roberta. She whispered something in her ear, but Roberta didn't hear it. She kept questioning. It's all she had. Questions without any satisfying answers. Her grandmother led her down the center aisle and everyone watched the reverse processional. The pastor only began speaking again as they were exiting the sanctuary into the foyer. The only words she heard were:

"… pray for this child …"

Roberta cried uncontrollably and her grandmother stooped to her knees and hugged her, Roberta's head softly tucked into the arc of the neck.

"Shhhh. It's okay, Roberta. Let it out. Let it all out."

They stood in the middle of the foyer, several eyes peering out from the sanctuary door. Two of them belonged to Mr. Goodwin, who parted the doors quietly and approached them.

"Mrs. Newsom, if you need a ride home, I'm happy to drive you."

"Thank you, but no, I don't think that will be necessary. Roberta, do you want to go back inside?"

"No, I want to go home."

"Well, I don't want to trouble you, Mr. Goodwin."

"Mrs. Newsom. I have my car, not my truck. There's plenty of room. I'll pull around front and wait for you out there."

"Thank you."

***

Roberta and grandmother sat in the back seat as Mr. Goodwin drove them home. Roberta was glad he didn't have his truck as she thought of the sack. Grandma Newsom kept her arm around the child and whispered things here and there. Some about letting out her feelings. Others about what Roberta would like to have to eat when they got home.

Roberta and Grandma worked in the kitchen. Little was spoken except for necessity. Roberta wondered what her mother was doing all alone at the church.

"When will Mom come home?"

"Maybe an hour."

By the time her mother arrived three hours later, early evening was beginning to settle into the town. The two mothers of the house discussed the memorial service.

"It was nice."

Nice, thought Roberta. *How could it be?*

Her mother didn't mention Roberta's early exit or outburst. All was acceptable. All feelings, all words, all actions.

They made a light dinner and settled into the living room for New Year's Eve 1944.

"Mom, can I stay up until midnight?"

"Yes."

Grandmother had a surprised look in her eyes

but didn't comment. Instead, she walked over to the wooden Westinghouse radio on the stand next to the Christmas tree. She turned the knob and the wiry noise of the airwaves curved through the room until the dial tuned into the local station.

"It's time for Great Gildersleeve. You wanna listen, Roberta?"

She nodded. It was her typical Sunday evening program. On this New Year's Eve edition, the Great Gildersleeve strapped on his skates with his nephew and niece and tried to get his balance on the frozen pond. As Gildersleeve crashed to the hard ice on his tubulars to the raucous laughter of the radio show's audience, Roberta turned to her mother.

"Mom, can you buy me some ice skates?"

"We have ice skates, Roberta. In the basement, I think. We probably even have your size."

"Can I use them?"

"I'll take you down to the lake to skate sometime."

"Tomorrow?"

"We'll see."

She thought of the freedom, standing on the edge of the lake and looking off to the other side. A free glide across, an adventure … to find … she wasn't sure, but she wanted to try.

Chapter 7

Rubber Bands & Ice Skates

A month after her father left for the war, Roberta played by herself in the house with a wooden toy truck that was cursed with a wheel which continually fell off. She had placed her doll inside the back of the truck and pushed it around with gusto until the same pesky wheel slid out of its socket and onto the floor. She picked up the wheel with great urgency and ran through the dining room into the kitchen.

"Mommy, my truck broke. Where's daddy—?"

Her mother turned around from the sink. No answer was needed when she saw Roberta's face falling from exuberance to understanding. She had forgotten for a moment. Just a moment.

She turned around and walked back into the living room carrying the wooden wheel in her hand. Her mother, without saying a word, continued washing the dishes.

***

On New Year's Day, Grandma emerged from the cellar steps carrying two pairs of ice skates—an adult one and a kid's one.

"Roberta?"

"Ice skates!"

She grabbed the pair from the clutches of her grandma and turned towards her mother in the other room.

"Mom, Grandma found the skates. Can we go skating? You said we could sometime."

Her mother sat on the sofa with a flipped open but empty notepad across her lap.

"Skating? Oh ..." Her face looked past Roberta to her mother standing in the doorway to the kitchen. "Not today, Roberta."

"But Mom, you said you'd take me."

"I didn't say today. Grandma, did you have to go digging these out?"

Grandma Newsom walked past Roberta near the edge of the kitchen doorway and held up the skates to her daughter. "Tricia, why not? It's a beautiful day."

"Beautiful?" The reply was sharp and terse.

Grandma paused with an impatient grin. "It's sunny out. About 32 degrees. It's a perfect day to try them out. Besides, it's the New Year. How about a little fun?"

"Fun?" The snap in her voice was the same.

"Tricia, please."

Roberta had never noticed the two women in the house speaking to each other like this before. She didn't like the fast tempers and the impatience, so she handed Grandma the skates.

"No, I don't want to skate. I'll go play in my room."

Her mother stood up immediately.

"No, Roberta. Your grandmother is right. We should go skating. Go put your long underwear on, and get your scarf and mittens."

"Really?"

"Yes, really."

Grandma handed the skates to the reluctant mother. "And I'll have some hot chocolate and cookies ready for the return."

An uncomfortable moment quickly became the best of days as Roberta smiled and bounded up the staircase to hunt for her long johns.

***

The lake lay in front of the two skaters like a pristine sheet of ice ready for them to explore. Her mother explained to Roberta how she fell in love with skating when she was young.

"Your Grandpa Newsom brought me here as a girl. Those are my old skates." She referred to the ones Roberta put on by the edge of the lake, sitting flat in the crusted snow.

"And I met your Daddy ice skating. Not here. Down near the center of town. There was a popular hangout and I met him when I was only fifteen. We skated many times over the years."

Roberta pictured her father in uniform, like the photographs she had of him in the house, on skates and twirling her mother around him in circles.

"What if I can't skate?"

"I'll teach you."

She reached down for Roberta's hands and helped her up. She wobbled.

"This feels weird."

"You have to get used to it. The first lesson is how to fall."

"Fall? I thought we were supposed to stay up?"

Her mother laughed. "Yes, but everyone falls, especially a new skater. But no matter how hard it hurts, you have to get back up."

"So how do I fall?"

"Lean to one side. Knees. Use your arms to help break the fall. Here, I'm going to let go."

Roberta's foot slipped out from under her, and she flopped backwards onto the edge of the ice.

"Owww!"

Her mother laughed. "I've done that more than once. Now onto your knees. Now one foot at a time. There you go."

Roberta went down again quickly.

"This is no fun."

"It will be, I promise. Here, take my hand. We're going to go."

Her mother grabbed both of her hands and began skating backwards, holding Roberta up on the ice until she started to feel more confident.

"I'm going to let go."

"No. Don't. I'm—"

She let go. Roberta stood on two metal blades and she moved slightly forward.

"I'm doing it."

"Yes, you are."

"I'm skating."

She hadn't noticed that they were already a hundred feet from the shore. She looked up for a moment and glanced across the open ice in front of her leading to the other side of the lake. She thought of her father, somewhere over there, and it almost felt like she could find him if she had the will to cross over with her newly found skill. She almost said something. Something about the other side. The view felt different from on top of the lake itself. And as she prepared to tell her mother what she was thinking, the skates gave way, and she landed on her side on top of the sheet of ice. She had fallen the right way, and it hadn't hurt. Not at all. And she pulled herself up and looked back at her mother in youthful exuberance.

"It didn't hurt."

"I told you."

"I want to learn to be a good skater. Like you and daddy."

"You will. Let's go."

"Mom?"

"Yes?"

"Did you ever skate across the lake?"

"The whole way? No. And you're never to do that, you hear?"

"Why not?"

"The further across the lake you go, the more dangerous. We don't know how stable the ice could be. It could get thin out there, and terrible things could happen."

Roberta thought of her father again.

"Like daddy? He went out across the lake and a terrible thing happened to him."

"Oh Roberta."

They spent the next hour enjoying a mother and daughter moment which had been missing since Christmas Eve. When they arrived home,

Grandma, true to her word, had the hot chocolate ready and the cookies in the oven.

"Mom?"

"Yes."

"Do you ever want to go over there?"

"Where?"

"Across the lake, where daddy's body is?"

Her mother didn't reply. Grandma paused for a moment and picked up a cloth pot holder to check on the cookies. A burst of warm air escaped, and Roberta felt the rush against her still cold thighs as she sat in her long johns.

"Mom, do you ever forget that daddy is dead? I sometimes do. When I was out on the lake, I felt like he was there. Somewhere."

Her mother reached across the table and put her hands on Roberta's, which were clenched around the warm mug.

"Yes, Roberta. I do forget sometimes."

"It doesn't seem real."

"Sometimes it doesn't."

"Can we go skating again tomorrow?"

"You're supposed to go back to school tomorrow."

"Mom, don't make me. Can I have one more day at home?"

It didn't take long for her mother to agree.

***

Her eyes were closed, but the image was real. The sun shone brightly. One of those vivid blue skies and the long days which make life feel like an eternity in one moment. She stood in the backyard and called out a word. It wasn't clear at first, but then she heard it correctly. She had half-cupped her mouth with her right hand to accentuate the yell.

"Trigger! Come boy, come!"

Trigger raced around the yard, zigzagging back and forth. He played keep away as the laughing child taunted him with zigzagged steps of her own.

Her laughter spilled over into her head, and it recycled itself with a contentedness that made her lips raise in a comfortable smile.

"Trigger."

The dog barked in delight.

The green of the grass provided a vibrant spring background to the terrier with so much life in each jump. It chased her until something strange caught her eye. It was on Trigger's leg. An attachment of sorts. Trigger continued playful barking from a few feet away, but Roberta's eyes zoomed in to the legs of the dog. Rubber bands. She identified it as a rubber band around

Trigger's leg. As she confirmed her sight, all of Trigger's legs had them. Rubber bands, multiple strands of them ran back and forth from each leg. As his legs moved, the bands moved. But then she noticed something. It wasn't the legs moving the bands, the rubber bands were moving the legs. They stretched and pulled and powered the dog forward. The dog couldn't do anything without the rubber bands. It was at that moment that she remembered that rubber bands don't move a dog's legs. *This isn't real,* she thought. *Trigger isn't alive. He's dead. And I'm dreaming.*

She opened her eyes and stared at the ceiling. Rubber bands. Dogs don't have rubber bands for legs. Trigger was dead. She remembered. She climbed out of bed and peered into the faint dawn of morning. Through the dim veil slowly lifting, she could see the wooden pole sticking out of the ground that confirmed everything she felt in her heart. She glanced to the space behind her door, and saw the skates sitting idly. She thought of the expanse of ice and the faint glimpse she had of the other side. Both her father and dog were still gone. She crawled back under the covers and allowed the warmth of the wool comforter to ease her back into a peaceful sleep for another few moments.

When she came downstairs for breakfast, she

intended to tell her mom and grandmother about the dream, but decided not to as her grandmother had something she wanted to tell Roberta.

"Roberta, your mom and I have been talking it over, and I'm going to be moving into your house with you full-time. Is that all right, Roberta?"

"Of course, Grandma. What will you do with your house?"

"I think maybe this spring I'll try and sell it. We can all be a happy family together. Doesn't that sound nice?"

There would be three of them. And no dog. The thought made her happy, but it didn't relieve the image of the bands wrapped tightly around Trigger's legs. She didn't want to tell them anymore.

Chapter 8

First Flight

Roberta learned ice skating in the freezing environment of January 1945. A cold front continued to accumulate snow on the ground. Wind whipped the swirls off the ice and what the wind didn't accomplish, mobs of youth and overgrown kids swept the lake for hockey games, figure eight skating, or just fun glides across the cold sheen.

After a few more lessons from her mother, Roberta had gotten permission to skate on the edge of the lake by herself with a few strict stipulations:

- One. Ask permission first.
- Two. Have a friend present
- Three. Be home before dark
- Four. Stay on the portion by the shore that her mother had shown her

By Mid-January, she glided skillfully across the ice, and she had a small rotating group of friends, mostly older, whom she would skate with after school and on weekends.

She had gotten used to the stares and whispers from kids at school upon her return.

"She's the girl whose father died in the war," she heard one say.

But as uncomfortable as those early stares were, they disappeared quickly, which was also a difficult concept for her to accept.

I still don't have a daddy, she would think. *I'm still the girl who lost her father in the war. The same as yesterday.*

But the conversation always shifted. "Roberta, do you want to skate after school?"

"Yes."

She wondered if one day she would forget to think about her father. Even the tone of the pastor had changed by the third week after the death. The sincere handshakes, accompanied by the hugs from the pastor's wife in the first couple of weeks, quickly became the stale "hellos" and the nod of the head as in the old days.

"Mom, can I go skating?"

"Who are you going with?"

"Patty."

She was the thirteen-year-old neighbor girl.

"All right but remember—"

"I know, stay by the edge."

The names might have changed, but the

conversation occurred in nearly identical fashion day after day.

After each skating session, Roberta would do two things. First, she would stare off across the lake for a final visual of the other side. Then, when she returned home, she would walk around to the back of the house and follow the snow path she created to the wooden pole sticking from the ground. She would talk to Trigger for a moment, often thinking of the rubber bands and the sack dripping with blood. She would tell him about school and about the happenings while skating.

"I wish you were on the ice with me."

She would close her conversation the same way. "Trigger, I'm sorry you don't have a stone like Grandpa Newsom but just wait until spring. We'll get you one, don't worry. We'll never forget."

This always made her think of her father as well, and she would slip into a momentary trance and think about the two souls no longer with her, without a stone to their names. They were still alive inside of her, and that was what mattered, she told herself.

The idea came to her slowly. It wasn't one thing in particular that gave her the resolve. A combination of factors contributed to her desire to do it. But there was a trigger to her action and that occurred one day when she heard a group of boys, all slightly older than her, discussing the war on the school bus.

"If they don't find the dog tags, then they don't know if someone died or not."

"Some soldiers have more than one dog tag."

"They do not."

"Yes they do."

"But without the dog tag, who knows whose body it is. They might have their head blown off and …"

She had never thought about the violence of war until that day. She had known that people fight, and she knew that it was far away, and she knew that soldiers died and didn't come back—her father's plane crash being one example. But when she heard "head blown off" she thought of how horrible that would look and she couldn't quite grasp what it all meant.

"Mom, what's a dog tag? Did Trigger have one?"

"Dog tag? Where did you hear about a dog tag?"

"Some boys on the bus were talking about dog tags, but I didn't understand."

"Dog tags are not for dogs. They are for soldiers."

Roberta cocked her head and thought how

funny it sounded.

"Then why ..."

Grandma Newsom, overhearing the conversation from the rear, stepped in with an explanation.

"Roberta, each soldier is given metal tags on a chain. Then if something happens to them, everyone will know who it was so they can tell their loved ones?"

"Like if their head gets blown off?"

"Roberta!" Her mother backed out of her chair with a shocked look. "Where did you hear that?"

"That's what the boys on the bus said."

"Don't talk like that. It's not polite."

"I'm sorry."

She felt confused, especially about her father.

"It's all right, Roberta," said Grandma. "This terrible war makes us talk about the most dreadful things."

"What happened to daddy's dog tags?"

They both remained silent.

"Is that how they knew it was daddy? They found his dog tags?"

Neither responded fast enough.

"How do we know that daddy was killed if we don't have his dog tags? Maybe they were wrong. Maybe he's still somewhere with the dog tags. Maybe—"

Her mother stood up and ran out of the room. Grandma took the seat at the table and placed her hand on Roberta's. "Roberta, your father is gone."

"I don't want him to be gone. He's still across the lake. I won't believe he's gone until I see his body in a coffin."

She stood up and ran upstairs to her room. She had witnessed a lot of quick exits, and this was her first. She sat on the bench by the window and looked out upon the back yard. The wooden pole caught her eye, and she stared at it out of respect or anger or disillusionment or all of the above. The frigid wind flapped the ends of the canvas covering the dwindling pile of firewood stacked against the wooden shed. A gust lifted the end flap of the canvas and loosened it enough for the entire piece to shoot up into the air and fly out of sight to the other side of the shed. Roberta stood up in a flash, ready to tell her mother, but the sight of the canvas in the wind, floating on its own made her think of her wings—the ones she received from the man in the uniform Christmas Eve. She turned her head and saw the metal wing sitting on the edge of her small desk. She walked over and placed it in her palm. This is when the idea came to her. It was time to fly.

***

One. Permission. "Mom, can I go skating?"

"Yes, who are you going with?"

Two. "Patty." She hadn't exactly talked to Patty about skating that day, but it was Saturday and she knew she would be there at some point.

Three. Before dark. Not a problem because it was morning.

Four. Stay near the shore. Well, skaters stay near the shore, but she wasn't skating that day. Not really. She had much bigger plans.

Before she left the house, she pinned the wings on the collar flap of her coat and looked into the mirror. She liked it. She felt important, like a pilot on a mission, like she was doing something for her country. She would discover the truth. She had to, for everyone, and if it meant that she had to break rule four, or even two for that matter, she felt confident that her mother would understand. And if she didn't, then her grandmother would for sure.

She traipsed across the street, skates slung over her shoulder, her father's wooden airplane in her hand, and sauntered into the unknown of her mind. What would she find? How long would it take? Would she be back by dark? She thought rule three was safe, but long journeys are sometimes best taken under the guise of darkness. She plopped herself on a stump by the edge of the lake and laced up her skates with the airplane in her lap. Between each pull and tie, she glanced out over the frozen water to the vast unknown barely visible on the other side. The overcast sky released meager flurries which fluttered to their unknown resting place, buoyed on by a persistent wind.

"The wind is good. It's at my back," she said.

No one else was there. She stood on her blades and wobbled onto the ice. She patted the wings on her left collar and peered into the expanse. She took a single deep breath, and making the sound of a roaring engine, lifted the airplane as high as she could and started skating into the wide-open. By this point, she had good balance and had increased her speed quite a bit compared with two weeks earlier. She alternated her view between the path of ice and the distant shore — the plane bobbing up and down in her hands. Within a minute she was out beyond the boundaries that her mother had set for her, but plenty of open ice lay to her front, much of it already explored by numerous skaters from the community. She could see the worn ridges from the other skaters, and she avoided bumps and ruts as best she could.

A few minutes out, she stopped and looked back, still clutching the toy plane in her hand. Her house set off the shore by a slow incline, looked further than it ever had before. Was this what her father felt when he was leaving and when he looked back at the house? She loved that house, and she would return before dark, but she had to keep moving.

"Don't look back anymore, Roberta. Stay focused."

She remembered the moth that she had watched fly out of sight. It had two wings, just like her. She raised the airplane into the sky. *Soar. Keep soaring. Keep moving.* She lunged forward and tripped over a hardened knob of ice. She fell face-first onto the hard surface, but undeterred, immediately regained her footing, scooped up the unfazed bi-plane and paced herself into the future. She pushed left then right, left then right.

The distant trees grew with each push of her leg and her eyes remained focused on them, completely obsessed with the reality they meant. Her mind, blank to all else, pushed her on further, further, further. That's when the surface gave way, like her heart had bottomed out and all drive and fortitude had been extinguished with the first dip of her right leg, followed by a slow fracturing crackle beneath her. She looked down. The veins of the ice spread in all directions with breakneck speed. Her heart pounded, and she looked frantically left and right for an escape from the splintering underneath her. She sided her right blade to a stop, but it pierced through the top of the ice into the water. Roberta fell to the side. Her mother's lesson on falling gracefully popped into her mind, but it had little meaning as the ice gave way. She screamed as the grip of fear tensed each muscle of her body. She felt alone, as a dead weight plunged with purpose to the bottom. Her father. *Was this what he felt? Plane going down all alone?* The images pulsed through her mind in an endless stream—airplane, wings, water, alone, sinking in the cold—and she fell back first, right foot already in the water, and her entire body slid through the frail ice into the deep. The water stung her cheeks as she gasped for breath. She flailed her arms but sunk further until she bobbed upward once, with arms flapping out of the surface. She managed another scream and breath before she lost herself below the water line. Darkness faded in on her. She wouldn't be home by dark. It was already dark. Her wings provided no help in the water, and she faded further, thinking lastly of her mother's face and then her father's smile the day he wore the uniform by the lake. Her mind turned blank, and she felt scared and alone for a second before she opened her eyes one last time and saw the beast. A white-winged

creature with long arms and two peering eyes. The wings spread out over top of her, and she felt like something was spinning a cocoon around her, like she was the butterfly not yet ready for flight, and a white-winged being was preparing her for the long winter months until a second attempt could be managed. She felt a pull and a tug and the white of its wings faded to darkness and she lost consciousness into the
arms of the unknown.

Chapter 9

Eyes Open

Coldness. A chill rippled down her arm. She saw beyond her closed eyes. A vision. A giant winged creature. White. Steady. Peering eyes. Almost human eyes. She heard herself cry for help, and the cold tingling of her arm felt a touch, then a tug. A harsh pull. The creature flapped its wings like the moth floating in its jagged pattern, left right, up down, unreachable in its flight for freedom. An unmistakable ability to elude all who chased it. Its flight lifted over the lake and as it flew into the pale backdrop of the dreary sky, it disappeared under the knowledge that it still survived and moved without the need for anyone's eyes to be upon it. It remained a part of the scene. An integral part of the horizon, forever fused into the mind as it flitted itself toward the trees on the opposite shore.

As the thought of the winged creature wrested her mind awake, Roberta opened her eyes slowly to a bright, white light. She couldn't tell if she was shivering in the water or if the white light led to another place. One of peace, perhaps. Maybe one where she could talk to daddy, and she could hold his hand. Someone was holding *her* hand. She now felt it. She shivered once more as a heaviness rested upon her. She wanted to lift her arm to shield her eyes from the bright white above her, but it felt too heavy. She felt too weak, so she waited for comprehension, which came in the form of a voice.

"Roberta."

It was her mother. She slightly lifted her head and moved her eyes down from her upward stare. Two familiar faces loomed over her. Mother and grandmother. A back wall came into view. White. Sounds of voices and clicking wheels and coughing and muted stale talk emanated around her and filled her ears.

"Roberta."

It was her mother's hand holding hers. She could now tell, but the scene, setting, and characters made no sense. She felt the pull of the water all around her and shivered once more. She no longer wore her skates. Even her clothing felt strange. Light. Funny.

"Oh, darling Roberta. You had us all so worried."

Her eyes focused beyond her mother for a moment. A woman with a nurse's cap pushed a cart down an aisle. The wheels clicked in a steady beat as it moved over the edged lines of the tile. The room was large with many beds in neat lines on both sides of the aisle. She saw old men and sick coughing women and two others closer to her age.

Both her mother and grandmother spoke to her. Each one grabbing a section of her arm, but Roberta's mind didn't comprehend their meanings. But as her senses galvanized inside her, she finally spoke: "Mom, what happened?"

Her mother was crying, so Grandma Newsom explained.

"You almost drowned, dear child."

She remembered skating. She remembered looking out across the lake and keeping her eyes on the other side as she weaved along the open trails. She also remembered the sinking feeling. She felt it again, at that moment, in her stomach. Helpless, and she glanced up once to the white ceiling as if she looked to the surface far above her, wishing for a way to reach it.

"I told you not to go out there alone," her mother snapped through her tears.

Grandma placed her arm on her daughter and motioned for her to slow down.

"I remember it being very white," said Roberta. "I fell in the water, and I saw something coming at me. All white. I was scared."

"Oh child," her grandmother rubbed her arm as her mother covered her face and sobbed.

"You were very fortunate, Roberta. It was like an angel was watching over you."

"An angel?"

"You were lucky you were not alone."

"I was the only one on the lake."

"No. Jed Travers saw you heading out towards the center. He said he knew the lake current kept that part of the ice unstable, and he followed you out. When you went under, he laid himself down on the edge of the ice to try and reach you. You came up to the surface twice, and he was able to grab your wrist, but the ice broke and he plunged into the water over you. He swam down and grabbed you and was somehow able to get you onto a stable patch of ice. Then he kicked his legs and was able to stretch out safely on top of the ice. You weren't responding, and he dragged you the whole way to shore and flagged down the first car to take you to the hospital. The hospital called us from there. Jed Travers saved your life."

Saved your life. Almost drowned. She thought.

Roberta knew who Jed Travers was. A young man in his twenties, he often passed the offering plate at church, and he worked at the Gulf Station down the street. Roberta remembered seeing him there when her mom would stop in for a fill-up. She had never seen him skating before. *He saved my life,* she repeated in her head.

This was when she recognized that she didn't have her clothes on, only a thin hospital gown, but she was wrapped in a heap of blankets that weighed her down—not dissimilar to the feeling of being unable to move in the water.

"Where are my clothes?"

Her mother had regained composure and had sat beside her on the edge of the bed. "Your clothes were soaking wet. You had lost consciousness and were freezing. They had to warm you immediately."

"They took my clothes off?"

"The nurses. Oh, Roberta, we were so afraid. What were you thinking?"

"I'm sorry, Mom."

"You better be."

"I broke rule number four. And number two, but—"

"There's no buts. What if I lost you? What if …" Her mother turned away. It was as if she ran out of the room. Grandma remained silent. "Roberta, I lost your father. I can't lose you too."

"I'm sorry. I wanted to get to the other side. I miss daddy."

Her grandma put her hand on Roberta's head and rubbed it.

"I just wanted to fly to the other side and see if I could find him."

"He's not there, Roberta. He's not on the other side of the lake. He's dead."

The tone was harsher than usual. Almost as cruel as the message her mother was giving.

"But Mom, Daddy said he was crossing the lake."

"It's not that lake. Roberta—"

Grandma Newsom told her mother to stop. Not with words but with a certain look.

A white-capped nurse inserted herself into the tension without knowing she did everyone a favor. Behind her stood a young man wrapped in a thick wool quilt.

"Well, I have someone who wants to see you, young lady. You've had quite the experience, and I think you should meet your guardian angel. I think you know him. Jed Travers."

The adults all nodded and greeted each other. Roberta's mother even gave the young man a hug, but she had to widen her reach around the thick blanket.

"How are you feeling?" he asked.

Roberta stared at him for a moment. His face was slightly red and both of his fists were balled up and clinging to the edge of the blanket on both sides of his chin.

"Roberta, don't you have something to say to Jed?" her grandma asked.

"Thank you."

"You're welcome. I'm glad I saw you out there. I know the lake pretty well, and once I saw you …"

He continued talking, but Roberta didn't hear any more of his words. She just stared at him. He looked healthy. Young. Younger than her father. And the question kept coming to the front of her mind. It didn't make any sense, so she decided to blurt it out.

"Why didn't you go to the war like my daddy?"

Everyone paused in silence for a moment. Jed chuckled a little and looked left to her grandmother then right to her mother with a slight nonchalant embarrassment crossing his slight grin.

"Well, I was planning on going …"

His explanation rambled on for a minute. She didn't understand it very well. It had something to do with his right eye. She looked at it. It seemed to be a normal right eye. But there was something wrong with it, because the army rejected him. Upon that realization, another thought occurred to her. If his eye had been normal, he would be across the lake like her father. If that was true, who would have saved her? Would she have drowned? Would she be dead?

"Do you have wings?" she asked, interrupting his army excuse.

"Wings?"

"I saw something coming at me in the water. It was white, and it had wings."

Jed laughed. "I've never had wings."

Wings, she thought. *The wings.*

"Well, it's a miracle," Grandma Newsom exclaimed. "It's like you were her guardian angel. My, my. What can we ever do to repay you?"

"I'm just glad I was there."

Roberta sat up straight in bed for the first time. An energy pulsed about her as she remembered that which was most important.

"The airplane. What happened to my airplane?"

She asked this question to Jed Travers. He looked confused.

"Airplane?" asked her mother.

"My airplane. The one daddy sent me for Christmas. Where is it?"

"You mean you had it with you on the lake?"

"I was flying my airplane across the lake. Where is it? Did you get it?" she asked Jed.

"No. I didn't see any airplane."

How could someone not see an airplane? she thought.

"It's a bi-plane. Red. With wings painted on it."

"I'm sorry. I didn't see it."

"My plane. Did you not see it because of your bad eye? The eye that made you stay home from war."

"Roberta," scolded her mother. "That's uncalled for."

"Mom, my plane went down in the lake. Mom. My plane."

"Roberta, we can get you another plane."

"It went down in the lake just like daddy went down. Can you get me another daddy?" The anger seeped from her voice and the words ripped silence across all of the adults. "I want my airplane. I want my daddy."

Her mother excused herself. Jed said a few sheepish things about how he was glad she was all right. Grandma Newsom thanked him again, and he left with the nurse. The two of them stared at each other—Roberta's eyes full of tears—and her grandmother held her hand.

"It's not fair, Roberta. It's not fair at all. But we also have to thank God for Jed Travers, because he saved your life today. It's going to be fine.

Everything will be fine. We'll get through this. I'll get you another plane."

"I don't want another plane."

"All right. That's fine. Everything's fine."

***

The hospital released her around four in the afternoon, and they went home. Roberta went to her room and sat alone on the bench, looking into the fading light of the backyard. Trigger's pole kept her attention more than anything else. Dead. She was almost dead like Trigger. Like her father. She wondered what death would have felt like. Would she have been happy like Pastor had said? Would she have been in a sack with blood dripping down? Would she have been in a coffin like Grandpa Newsom? Nothing felt real, except the blanket which she wrapped around her shoulders.

"Roberta, wash-up for dinner," called Grandma's voice from downstairs.

"All right."

She thought of the plane floating in the water, maybe flying now on its own, and she hoped it would find her father, and if not on the other side, then at a happy reunion in heaven.

Chapter 10

The Jed Travers Incident

Men. Everywhere. She thought they all had gone off to war. But Roberta began noticing the men all around her. Mr. Dwyer and his leg issue. Mr. Goodwin and his truck which kills animals. Pastor Jenkins and his weekly sermons. Mr. Tenney, her gym teacher. Why wasn't he physically fit enough for war? And then there was Jed Travers and his bad eye. Everyone had a good excuse. Or at least a military approved excuse. Except daddy, she thought. She couldn't understand why fate—a concept she literally didn't understand—had chosen to take her father beyond the lake and never allow him to return.

The maligned eye remained in her mind. What was wrong with Jed Travers' eye? She wanted to know. But how?

On a Saturday morning in late January, Roberta sat in the backseat of their four-door Mercury sedan as mother drove to the grocery store. They pulled into the Gulf Station less than a mile down the road. The pavement around the pump had been cleared, but snow piles on all sides created a hedged-in, snow-globe environment. Jed Travers exited the service office, buttoned up his jacket and came alongside the driver's window. Her mother rolled it down halfway.

"Hello, Mrs. Ares."

"Hello, Jed."

"Fill'er up, ma'am?"

"Yes, thank you."

She rolled the window up as Jed walked to the back of the car, flipped up the license plate, removed the cap, and inserted the hose to begin pumping. He used a squeegee to clean off the salt residue from all the windows. When he came to Roberta's back window, he waved to her, but she didn't wave back. She concentrated on his right eye, tilting her head and placing her face against the window as if it was a magnifying glass. The eye looked normal.

With the windows clean, he popped open the hood. Roberta unlatched the door and slipped into the cold.

"Roberta, where are you going?"

She shut the door but not tight. She didn't want to make a noise. She crept along the side of the car, past her mother's window. Her mother spoke something through the glass, but didn't roll it down. Roberta kept her eyes on the back of the raised hood and slowly peeked around its edge. She could see the partial right side of Jed's face as he inspected the dipstick in his hand. Could he really not see her? Was he blind in that eye? In her mind, she could prove everything once and for all. If he only noticed her when she was in view of his left eye, then she would know that there was a real problem and that was why he hadn't gone to war and—

Before she could properly test the theory. Slam! The hood crashed down into its slot like a collapsing building. The edge of the hood faintly nipped the tips of two of her fingers which clung on to the side panels of the car. She screamed and Jed almost tripped over the concrete ledge of the pump.

"Roberta! I didn't see you there."

Roberta's mother whipped open the car door.

"Roberta! What are you doing?"

"I—" She didn't rightly know.

"I'm sorry, Mrs. Ares. I didn't see her there with the hood up. Roberta, did the hood get you? Are you alright?"

"I'm fine."

"Roberta, what were you doing?" asked her mother.

The girl turned around and climbed back into

the car and shut the door.

"I'm sorry, Jed. I don't know what's gotten into her."

"Not a problem, Mrs. Ares. $2.55 for the gas, ma'am."

"I'll get that for you."

They drove out of the Gulf Station without any answers.

***

Second attempt. Undeterred, a few days later as her grandmother drove the car and Roberta slid into the open freedom of the backseat, as she typically did, she needed an excuse and in a hurry.

"Grandma, I have to go to the bathroom."

"Roberta, we just left the house. Can't you hold it?"

"No, Grandma. It's an emergency. I have to go."

"Well, you'll have to wait until—"

"Look, Grandma! The Gulf Station. I can go there. Please. I have to go!"

"All right," she sighed.

The Mercury pulled in alongside the window to the tiny office. Roberta opened the door and paused for a moment, looking back across the trunk of the car to her target, Jed Travers, pumping gas and servicing the car under the hood.

"Roberta, I thought you said it was an emergency," Grandma Newsom stated, as she observed the sudden non-action of the person who a minute ago nearly exploded.

"Oh yes." Roberta turned and ran around the back of the station. She opened the bathroom door to at least go through the motions, but the smell repulsed her backwards. "I'm not going in there." She crawled along the wall and peeked out from the corner of the building right at the rear end of the Mercury. She crouched and slid behind the idling car, then sprinted across the pavement, avoiding several icy spots, until she hunched herself behind the car Jed filled. She looked back once at her grandmother, who stared at her in disbelief from behind the window of the driver's seat. Roberta knew she only had a moment before her grandmother would roll down the window and ask what in the tarnation she was doing. She had to act with haste.

She twirled around the back end of the car, slid under the pump hose attached to the car's gas tank, and ran full speed directly smack-dab into the center of Jed Travers standing at the window of the customer's car. Jed released a surprised yelp, and Roberta backed away and looked straight up as if staring at the cliff of a mountain.

"Roberta! What are you doing?"

Panic struck her mind, and without saying a word, she zigzagged around Travers like a fullback in the open field, circled around the front of the car, and dove into the back seat of the Mercury.

"Go, Grandma, go."

"What in the tarnation are you doing?"

"I don't need to go."

"What were you doing over by the pump?"

"Ah, asking for the key."

"Did you get it?"

"What?"

"The key?"

"No."

"Well?"

"Well what, Grandma?"

"Don't you have to go to the bathroom?"

"No, I was wrong."

"You were wrong?"

"Yes. I don't have to go. It went away."

"It went away?"

"Let's go, Grandma. We don't want to be late."

She sighed, put the car in first, and pulled out of the service station. Roberta had plastered her face to the backseat window and stared at Travers as the car passed the pump. Jed waved, but Roberta didn't respond. She had no more proof that Jed wasn't fit for the army. In fact, all she proved was that he saw better than she did since she was the one who ran at a dead sprint right into him.

She became obsessed every time they were in the car. "Can we stop at the Gulf Station?"

"Why?"

"Don't we need gas?"

"No."

"The windshield is dirty."

"I'm not stopping to clean the windshield."

"Why not?"

"The cleaning is a service you get when you buy something, not when you just pull in for a windshield cleaning."

"That's dumb."

She watched the Gulf Station go by.

"Can we stop at the Gulf Station?"

"Why?"

Pause.

"Roberta, why?"

"I just like it."

"What a strange child you are."

She watched the Gulf Station go by.

She was dissatisfied about the frequency of stops, so she realized she would have to take matters into her own hands. Before a certain trip to the grocery store, Roberta told her mother she'd be out in the car. She had a fool-proof plan. She walked to the driver's side front tire, bent over and removed her mittens. She twisted off the black cap of the tire valve and pressed down the flat round tip of the valve core until she heard a *psst*. She tried it again: *psst*. She ripped a barren twig from one of the bushes lining the driveway and poked it down into the core. *Pssss—tt.* Air escaped. She felt proud of herself.

"Roberta! What are you doing?"

She felt the looming presence of her mother over her back. She released the twig and the pressure from the core popped it into the air a few inches. She had no time to lose. She needed a response.

"Mom, look. The tire is low."

Her mother appeared on her left side and stooped down.

"It does look a little low. Why is the cap off the valve?"

"Oh, I did that," said Roberta.

"Why?"

"I was trying to blow air into the tire." She leaned over and put her lips on the valve.

"Roberta! You can't do that."

"You can't?"

"What am I going to do with you, girl?"

"Well, you could take me to the Gulf Station to get the tire pumped."

"Get in the car. But put the cap on the valve. And no more sucking the car."

"Yes, Mother."

They pulled into the Gulf Station. Old John Sloan, the owner, stepped out of the shop to inquire of Mrs. Ares. Another man. With some sort of infirmity. This one was simply old age, guessed Roberta. But her mind didn't stick with the reason for Mr. Sloan not defending Pearl Harbor and for focusing on those war-time essentials like pumping tires, she panicked about not seeing Jed. An elaborate plan to flatten the tire almost spoiled itself when she finally saw him walking around the edge of the building from the location of the bathroom. Quick. What to do? She remembered the old box of trinkets her father had left in the trunk. Various tools and spare parts and one sporting goods item: a baseball. Catch. Yes. She had the idea. Her mother had gotten out of the car and both Sloan and her chatted about the tire as Jed walked past the car, waved to

Roberta in the back seat, and circled around the front of the hood. She heard him say, "I'll take care of it, Mr. Sloan." Roberta sprang into action. She leaned into the front seat, extending her reach with her right hand while balancing her body with her left. Her fingers grabbed the key chain and yanked the key from the ignition. She inched her way backwards into her seat and snuck out the right-side door. She quietly popped open the trunk and peeked in at the box sitting in the right-side corner. She grabbed the baseball and hunched down behind the trunk lid which clicked loudly into place.

"Roberta?" her mother called.

Roberta stepped into the open. Jed stood in front of her mother looking down at the tire, holding an air pump in his right hand. His profile view hid most of the view of her mother except for the flailing lines of her winter coat and her stylish hat.

As Roberta yelled, "Jed, catch," and tossed the ball underhand on a looping path in the air, Jed had just dipped his head to attach the pump to the tire valve. The ball passed right over top of Jed's body and hit Roberta's mother right square in the nose.

The yell was unmistakable. Roberta stood paralyzed, staring at the shocked look on her mother's face. Jed had fallen over on his side, scared from the loud scolding behind him. He saw the baseball at his feet and picked it up.

"What happened?"

Roberta's mother still glared at her daughter, who was as stiff as a January snowman. "Roberta Jane! Why did you do that?"

She meekly raised her shoulders in an exasperated non-verbal "I don't know." Her mother continued to scold her as she ordered her in the car. Jed told Mrs. Ares that she could wait in the car too as he'd be done in a moment. Her mother sat down and reached for the keys in the ignition.

"Where are the keys?" She turned toward the backseat. "Roberta!"

A look of horror spread across Roberta's face as she remembered what she had done. "They are in the trunk."

"In the trunk? Why are they in the trunk?"

Raised shoulders again.

"Locked in the trunk?"

Her shoulders remained up with down-curved lips on her face. She couldn't imagine a way out of this one. Her mother asked her a series of questions related to the baseball bruise on her face and the keys locked out of reach. Roberta never explained, no matter how much her mother pried—exactly what Mr. Sloan did to the trunk. He used a crowbar to pry open the back to retrieve the keys. He tied down the trunk, which no longer latched properly, and told Mrs. Ares to bring the Mercury back next week, and he would replace the lock to the trunk.

Roberta heard an earful all the way to and from the store. She heard it all again in the presence of her grandmother around the dinner table. But not a single explanation emerged as she drifted off to sleep that night, no closer to solving the mystery of Jed Traver's eye.

***

The final attempt. Two weeks after the keys in the trunk incident. Roberta had another opportunity to investigate the eye during a routine gas fill-up. Instead of being sneaky, she decided to walk quietly up to the side of the open hood. She would flash her hands silently to see if his right eye would be able to see her. She would add a little more action and movement as needed until he recognized her. Of course, she had to escape the watchful eye of her mother, but instead of trying to explain, she just opened the door and walked up the left side of the car after Jed had opened the hood. Her mother knocked on the glass to grab her attention but to no avail. She peeked around the edge of the hood and spread her jazz hands wide like a vaudeville dancer, with sudden movement back and forth. Jed jumped back with a grunt. His right arm, which hadn't yet slipped the hood rod into the support slot, gave way and the hood crashed upon his head in conjunction with the side of his foot slipping off a patch of ice. Jed's head hit the side front of the car frame, with the hood smashing on top of him, until the force of the ice slip twisted his body further, and his entire frame slammed into the pavement as the hood snapped into place, once again just inches from both Roberta's and Jed's hands. Roberta's mother and grandmother hurried out of the car and circled to the front. They leaned over Jed, whose eyes were open, but dazed.

"My goodness, are you alright?" asked Grandma Newsom.

"Did you hit your head?" asked Roberta's mother.

His response was slow. "Yes. I … Roberta scared me. I didn't see her coming, and I lost the grip of the hood and fell on the ice."

"Do I need to call the doctor?"

"No, I'm all right." He propped himself up on his elbows with a wince in his eyes.

Roberta stood at his feet, staring, readying herself for the imminent eruption from her mother. Sure enough. Her mother stood up, and turned toward the silent conspirator.

"Roberta Jane. How can you justify your disgraceful behavior?! Why have you been torturing Mr. Travers? He's the one who saved you in the lake. You almost drowned. And he saved you, and all you've been doing is playing practical jokes on him, and look what you've done! You've hurt him. The man who saved your life. You should be ashamed of yourself. I'm ashamed of your behavior. Do you have any conceivable explanation for your disgraceful actions?"

Roberta let loose. The emotions exploded as tears covered her face. She sobbed and tucked her tears into her coat sleeves.

"You should be crying. You should be sorry. Why, Roberta? Why?"

Her head bobbed from the deep breaths as she choked on thoughts. The only ones that mattered. The eye. The white-winged creature which dove under to save her. It had such precision. It knew where to look and how to find her. It grabbed her arm and pulled her to the surface. It, beyond anything or anyone else, should have been the one at war. It had the will to fight, to struggle, to see the vulnerable, and to rescue the drowning. There was nothing wrong with the eye, as far as she could tell, except that it was used to pump gas at a time when it might be used to look through the scope of a rifle.

"I just wanted to know …" She managed to say through her cracked voice and wet face.

"What, Roberta?"

"What's wrong with your eye? Why couldn't you go to war? Why did my daddy have to go? But not Mr. Sloan, or Mr. Goodwin. Not Pastor Jenkins or my gym teacher. What's wrong? I just wanted to know what's wrong with your eye?"

She exhaled in a full body cry. Her mother sighed once and walked over to hug her. Jed stood up and approached Roberta.

"Roberta. I don't want to be here. I don't like it that every man my age is off fighting for our country, but I'm here. Stuck here." His voice became aggressive. "And I have to pump gas and think about the mundane life of our town while my friends are placing themselves in harms way every day. And they're doing it for me. And your father." He choked up and wiped a single tear from his eye. "Your father lost his life for his country. It should have been me. I should be there, but this eye." He pointed to it. "I injured it as a child. Everything is blurry, very blurry in this eye. So when I went to enlist in the army, they rejected me."

Roberta glanced up at him. Surprised. "You tried to join the army?"

"I sure did. I tried four times, but they rejected me every time. I'd give anything to go."

She reached towards him and wrapped her small arms around his mid-section. "Thank you, Jed Travers. Thank you for saving me."

He patted her head. "You're welcome."

"If you had gone to war, I wouldn't be here. Thank you."

He smiled. A smile of realization. As if part of the angst about his right eye had dissipated. As if part of the grand scheme of his life had been solved. Both Roberta's mother and grandmother hugged Jed and made sure he was all right. Roberta walked towards the backseat, and Jed called to her.

"I'm sorry I didn't find your airplane."

"It's all right. I'll find it. I won't give up. Just like you won't give up trying to join the army."

Neither Mother nor Grandmother questioned the behavior of Roberta again, and Roberta agreed in her mind that Jed Travers did indeed belong in her hometown. *He isn't right for war*, she thought. *He's meant to pump gas.* What she really meant was that he was the right man to save her.

He fought the war at home and had won a significant battle. That was enough for Roberta.

Chapter 11

Grandma Moves In

Over the next few cold and drab weeks, as the calendar moved into mid-February, Roberta continued to insist on stopping at the Gulf Station on a regular basis. No one minded. Her mother would pull in alongside the shop, whether needing gas or not, and Roberta would roll down her window and hand Jed a fresh baked good from Grandma's magical repertoire. She would wish him a good day, occasionally asking if he'd attempted to join the army again, and waved to him out the back window as the Mercury pulled into the street.

"He's like my angel," she said one day.

"That he is," her mother said.

"I was mean to him."

"Not anymore."

"Do you think he forgave me?"

"After that first muffin with cocoa? Yes, I'm certain of it."

***

Shortly after the Jed Travers' incident, Grandma Newsom asked Roberta to sit at the kitchen table to discuss an issue. Her mother loomed in the background.

"Roberta, remember how I told you I was going to sell the house and move in here?"

"Yes, Grandma, I remember."

"Well, I just sold my house. It became final yesterday."

"You sold your house?"

"Yes, so you're stuck with me full-time. I have nowhere else to go," she chuckled.

"Good, I wouldn't want you anywhere else. And Grandma, you'll keep teaching me how to make cookies?"

"Of course, sweetheart."

Her mother walked behind Roberta and sat down to her left. Roberta couldn't decide what Mother was thinking. She had a curious scowl on her face that fluctuated from tension and fake happiness. She knew her mother had something to say, or more precisely, something to add.

"Roberta," her mother started. "One of the reasons I asked your grandma to move in with us was because I'm starting a job."

"A job?"

"Yes. With your father gone, we need extra money. Grandma will be able to take care of you whenever I'll be at work."

"Where?"

"I'm going to be a teller at the bank. I start next Monday. How do you feel about me working?"

"Do I have to continue going to school?"

"Of course."

"So you'll be at work and I'll be at school?"

"That's right. And Grandma will be at home."

"And I'll have dinner waiting for both of you," Grandma added with a smile.

"All right. I'm all right with you working."

Her mother smiled and put her hand on the girl's arm. "Thanks for understanding, Roberta. We've had a lot of changes these past months, but we'll always have each other. And we'll stick together as a family, and ..." Her mother stood up. Tears in her eyes. "Excuse me."

"Mom?"

She stopped. "Yes."

"Do you want to work?"

There was a long pause.

"Yes, it will be nice to be out of the house. Meet new people."

"I'm glad you're working then."

"Thank you, Sweetheart."

"Can I visit you at work someday?"

"Maybe. Excuse me for a moment."

"Mom, why are you crying?"

"I don't know, Roberta. I don't know."

She left the room.

"Well," said Grandmother. "Tomorrow we're all going to my house to collect all the items I want to keep. I'm going to have an auction to sell everything else."

"An auction?"

"Yes, people come and bid on what they want. So … you ready to work tomorrow?"

"Yes, Grandma."

***

The Newsom house had been nearly dormant for the two months after the news of Mr. Ares' death. Grandma Newsom had only spent a handful of nights at her home during that time and had decided to sell the place around the end of January. It was a small house in town with a detached single car garage and a sizable back yard. Roberta used to spend a lot of time there when she was much younger, when Grandpa Newsom was still alive, but she hadn't been in a while when the three of them pulled into the driveway. Some of the snow had melted, but pockets of hardened, crusted white stuff still spread out across the yard. The walkway to the house hadn't been shoveled, and they plodded through the snow toward the back door.

"Roberta, do you see the fence back there?"

"Yes, Grandma. That's the flower bed."

"Yes, but I never told you that the fence used to be enclosed. That was Ginger's pen. After Ginger died, your grandpa removed the front of the fence and I put in a flower garden. He kept the backside to help keep away animals."

"I'm going to go look at it."

"All right."

Her mother and Grandma went in the house, and Roberta traipsed over the snow, which crackled like she stepped on shells. She put her hands on the first pole of the fence. It made her think of Trigger's pole, and she wondered why Ginger never had a pole to commemorate her. Or perhaps the fence was the way to remember Ginger. She thought of the poor dog, huddled in the straw, on a day much like the current one, and she imagined Grandpa Newsom finding the dog not moving or breathing. A heavy feeling fell on her stomach. She thought of Trigger's body cold and buried underground in the frozen dirt. Why was it all so gruesome? Almost wrong. Nearly evil. Why do things end? There were no philosophical components to these profound feelings. They simply effused from her body in the presence of yet another death to be remembered.

She turned from the fence and walked into the house, removed her boots, and ran into the living room calling for anyone who would listen. Her grandmother called back and descended the steps carrying a picture frame.

"Roberta, here it is."

"What?"

"The photo. I'd like you to have it if you still want it."

The gold framed grainy photo showed Grandpa Newsom in his green checkered shirt, sitting in a wooden rocker with Trigger plopped across his lap as if he had no energy.

"Thank you, Grandma. I love it."

She gazed at it. She had almost forgotten the features of Grandpa Newsom's face. The strong square jaw and the puffed cheeks with large eyes. Trigger looked peaceful. Happy. The way he used to look when sleeping at the foot of her bed every night until the accident.

"Grandma?"

"Yes, darling."

"Where's the rocker from the photo?"

"It's up in my bedroom. You want to see it?"

They ascended the steps. Her mother was stacking piles of clothing into a cardboard box in the hallway. They walked past her and into the last bedroom on the left. Sure enough, the rocker sat in the corner, and Roberta scooted into it without barely touching her feet on the floor. She held the frame with both hands and shifted her legs back and forth to move the chair.

"Grandma?"

"Yes."

"What are you going to do with this chair?"

"I'll sell it in the auction."

"Can I have it?"

"Oh, you want it?"

"For my bedroom."

"If it's all right with your mother, it's all right with me."

Her mother called from down the hallway. "What does she want?"

"Can Roberta have grandpa's rocking chair for her bedroom?"

"It's fine with me."

"Roberta, you can have it."

She rested her head on the back cushion of the chair. The photo rested on her lap. She was happy to have a photo of her dog and now a place to nurse his memories.

"I have to go help your mother."

"Grandma?"

"Yes?"

"Why did Grandpa Newsom want me to have the dog? Didn't he love it anymore?"

Grandma had the sweet smile of a saint as she walked into the room and sat on the edge of the bed next to the rocker.

"He loved Trigger very much."

"Then why did he give him to me?"

"I'll tell you."

Her mother peeked around from the edge of the door frame and listened in.

"When he heard that your father was going off to war, he knew you'd be alone with your mom, and he thought that you would love having Trigger in the house."

"But didn't he miss him?"

"He sure did, but …" Her grandma hesitated. "Let me tell you. You're old enough. You've done a lot of growing up recently, and you've handled everything so very well. At the time your father left, Grandpa Newsom was very sick. He couldn't take care of Trigger anymore, and I had to take care of your grandpa. So it was hard for me too. He had the idea to bless you with Trigger. And you took such good care of him. You made your grandpa very proud. When he passed later that year, he knew that Trigger would have a very good home indeed."

Roberta thought for a moment. The image that

came into her mind was Mr. Goodwin's truck sitting beside the body of the dog in the snow.

"But I didn't take good care of him. He died."

"Oh, no. No. You mustn't think that way. It wasn't your fault. Bad things sometimes happen. That's an unfortunate part of life. He would have been so proud of how you loved Trigger, and now how you remember him."

"We're still going to get a stone for Trigger, right? When spring comes. Like you said, Mom?"

Her mother nodded from the door. "Of course, we will."

Chapter 12

Spring Thaw

After nearly drowning, Roberta never used her skates again that winter. Her mother forbade her from getting on the ice, but Roberta herself had developed a healthy fear of the lake. She would, however, walk its edge and gaze out over the water, sometimes frozen, sometimes not. Her gaze never much lifted from the distant tree line on the far side. She remembered the free feeling of speeding towards it on her skates, believing that nothing would be able to stop her. The entire near-death incident replayed back in her mind often. She remembered the helpless feeling of falling, and the frigid jabs of the cold surrounding her entire body. And the darkness closing in as the white-winged creature salvaged her from the depths. She continued to question the creature. Was it Jed Travers? Was it something else? Or was it both?

An unseasonably warm and sunny March day brought an official end to winter, at least in everyone's mind. The thaw had sprung. Leftover piles of snow still lined driveways and road sides, but the lawns had been revealed. Roberta sloshed through the soggy soil to the edge of the lake completely free of ice once again. A realization came to her that day. She understood that her father wasn't actually on the other side of the lake. For the first time, the lake was a metaphor, though she didn't understand what that meant. The first moment she realized this, a tear fell across her cheek, and she had an extraordinary moment of loss. Like she truly would never see him again. Even her memories of his face had morphed into a mix of the photos of him her mother had displayed in the house. She felt she was losing him, in a final and absolute sense, after two and a half months.

"No," she screamed at the water, as if it had been to blame. "Why did you take him?"

It hadn't, but she said it anyway. She picked up a rock wedged in the mud and threw it into the water.

"Did that hurt you?"

No one else was around. She glanced back at her house a way off up the hill and across the road. She glimpsed her mother walking around the corner of the house, surveying the newly sprung crocuses. Earlier, Roberta had noticed them popping up and ran in to tell Mother and Grandmother. Both of them walked out onto the porch in the brisk morning air to inspect them.

"New life. That's why I love spring," said her grandma.

Spring. Life. It felt to Roberta that spring merely disrespected death, and death still hung over her eyes with every waking minute.

"No," she yelled again. "I never want to see you." She spoke to the distant shore line. "I will never go there. There is nothing there to see. I don't believe you."

Her few tears turned to anger, and she picked up whatever rocks and twigs she could and tossed them into the water. She wanted nothing to do with spring, and she prayed a simple prayer for the ice to return before she gathered herself together and went home.

That evening, around the supper table, she told them her revelation.

"Why did Daddy lie to me?"

Both her grandma and mother jerked backwards in surprise. Roberta had never spoken a bad word about her father before.

"He never lied to you," said Mother.

"Yes, he did. He told me that he was crossing the lake. And that he would be on the other side, and one day he would return. But he didn't cross the lake, did he?"

Both of the women sighed silently. Their

bodies told the story. The truth. Roberta could read it clearly. He did lie.

"He didn't lie. You were younger when he left. He wanted to explain what it would be like when he was separated from you."

"Roberta," her grandma interjected. "He actually went across the Atlantic Ocean. You know about this, right?" Roberta nodded. "So he used our lake here to help explain what was happening. It was a visual. Something that you could look at and remember your father."

Silence permeated across the table.

"His body is not on the other side of the lake," Roberta stated flatly.

"No," confirmed her grandmother.

"Is his body across the Atlantic Ocean?"

"Yes."

"Where?"

"We don't know."

"Why don't we know? How do we know that Daddy died?"

"Sweetheart, we've talked about this—"

Her mother stood up and ran out of the room. An eternal pause sat upon the kitchen table. A voice spoke in Roberta's head. It said that things would always be like this. She believed it.

"Did I say something wrong?" she asked her grandmother.

"No, sweetheart. Not at all."

***

The next morning at church, Pastor Jenkins preached a boring and long sermon. No one passed her mints anymore. She thought about Grandpa Newsom and how he used to nudge her with an open hand with two round mints placed in the middle. She would scoop them up, and they occupied her mind for the next few minutes. She could imagine the image of her grandfather even more than her father, or so it seemed. She wallowed deep in the memory of the mints when the first phrase from the sermon seeped into her consciousness.

"… when Christ returns, the dead shall live again …"

The dead will live again? Her first thought was of Trigger. *Will dogs live again too? How can the dead live again. When will Christ return?* She didn't bother to listen to the pastor's explanation when she had more than enough thoughts to parse out on her own. *The dead shall live. Daddy? Isn't he already in heaven?* she thought. *That's what the pastor had said to her before. His body lies in an unknown location, but he's also in heaven. And now he's also going to live again?* The messy contours of her thoughts swerved and merged on each other until one last phrase from the pastor stole her away from herself: "Bodies will rise out of the grave, the resurrection will occur, and the saints will meet their Maker in the sky."

The rhetoric confused her thoroughly. Especially the part about the bodies rising, and she grilled Mother and Grandma with the particulars on the way home. After all, Mother couldn't run away if she was driving the car. She had to answer.

"But Grandma, if nobody knows where daddy's body is, how will he be resurr—" She searched for the right letters.

"Resurrected."

"How can Daddy's body be resurrected if he's not in a grave? If nobody knows where his body is?"

"God knows."

"Why doesn't God tell somebody, so he can be buried?"

Neither of them had an answer.

After she peppered Sunday dinner with additional similar questions, she wandered to the lake once more. Perhaps to make peace with it. It hadn't done anything wrong, after all. It was just a lake, and she still loved the water, even though it tried to take her. She had picked up a stick and was flipping the water with its end, singing a melody from a Sunday hymn stuck in her mind when a single glance to her left revealed its answer. The water had spoken. The universe had given a response. Her wooden airplane lay overturned, bobbing up and down on the ripples of the water. One of its wings was tucked under the edges of a small rock. She lunged at it and snatched it out of the water. She held it with both hands in front of her face. A miracle was what popped into her mind. A resurrection. She raised her eyes over the expanse of the water and looked at the far shore and the puffed patches of branches reaching heavenward into the blue sky. She knew at that moment that it wasn't over. It couldn't be. Not now. Not after the airplane returned. Not after the pastor's sermon.

"Thank you. I won't give up. Ever."

She said it to the water, or maybe to the distant shore line. She might have even said it to heaven. Or all three.

"Mom! Grandma!"

She ran through the matted brown grass which had yet to sprout its spring greenness. She crossed the road even without looking—exactly how Trigger had done it. She ran into the house without even removing her wet and soiled boots.

"Mom! Grandma!"

"Roberta, don't traipse the mud through the living room," her mother said.

"Look! The airplane. It came back."

Grandma came down the steps to see the commotion. Her mother walked out from the kitchen.

"The airplane. My airplane. Daddy's airplane. The one he bought for me. The one I lost. It came back. It came back!"

They were all happy and amazed at the way the lake returned it to its rightful owner.

"Don't you see what this means? I was wrong. I'm going to get to the other side of the lake. I'm going to find Daddy. He's alive. Just like Pastor Jenkins said. Resurrected. Like this airplane. It's a sign. It has to be."

Neither of the women said anything, likely unwilling to remove the exuberance from the face of the girl. It would have been cruel to do so. Though cruelty would not leave forever. The harsh reality would one day set in permanently. Just not today. Not when she held her father's airplane in her hands once again.

Chapter 13

The Rock

Spring fully arrived, complete with the budding of flowers, the greening of the grass, and the flight of the birds soaring over the water, much like the wish Roberta had in her own heart. She knew the time had come to mention it. How could she not? They had promised, after all. So when she exited the grocery store and saw him coming out of the hardware store next door, she broke away from her mother to face him directly.

"Mr. Goodwin—"

"Hello, Roberta," he interrupted. Her mother had noticed the confrontation and followed Roberta from behind.

She didn't want to be cut off. Business had to be settled.

"I want to ask you about the rock."

"The rock?"

"Trigger's rock. The one you said you would help with after the weather got better." She looked straight up into the azure sky as an emphatic exclamation point to her plainly put sentiment. The weather screamed for it to happen. *He had to have noticed,* she thought. "Isn't it nice weather today?"

"Sure is, but—"

This time she would cut him off.

"You told my mother that you would get a rock and a plaque for Trigger, remember?" The 'remember' had attitude that emphasized any fool could have remembered something as basic as that. "Do you remember?"

"Roberta, your manners." Mother stood over her with a scowl on her face.

"And what about the manners of someone who doesn't do what he says?" she snipped.

"Roberta! Apologize to Mr. Goodwin right now!"

"No, it's alright ma'am. Roberta's right. The weather is fine, and it's about time that dog received the memorial it deserves. I'll tell you what," he looked right at the small girl. "Why don't you write out what you'd like the memorial to say. Your mother can give it to me, and I'll put it on the plague. I'll also find a nice stone to put in the ground. It will look swell. How's that?"

She nodded. Seemed sensible. Finally, the adults were seeing things the way they should. Her mother discussed with him a few details about the memorial, but Roberta's mind was already on the words. What should it say? She would spend the afternoon writing.

She cradled a small notebook in her hands as she rocked back and forth on Grandpa Newsom's rocker beside her bed. She occasionally glanced at the photo of him and Trigger on the table by the window. Her sacred task was clear: write a fitting tribute for Trigger.

Her first attempt: Trigger was a good dog.

Second attempt: Daddy gave me Trigger when he went to war.

Third attempt: Grandpa Newsom gave me Trigger when Daddy was going to war.

Fourth attempt:

She learned the tricky pitfalls of writing. The blank white page will often embarrass the forlorn eyes which stare at it. She needed it to be perfect, and her mother told her it had to be short. How to say it all in just a few words? How to commemorate a dog which was more than just a pet?

She left her rocker, sat on the bench by the window, and looked out at the pole sticking up from the ground. The soft spring soil had tilted it towards the house. With her pencil in hand, she wrote: *For Trigger. The best dog. From the best dad and the best grandpa. I miss you all.*

She had finished.

Her mother gave the paper to Mr. Goodwin, not without a sobbing fit when she read it, and not without hugging Roberta for an uncomfortably long time and telling her how meaningful it was.

Three weeks later, the rock delivery occurred. It was a Saturday afternoon, and Mr. Goodwin pulled his truck into the driveway. Two other men were with him. Roberta recognized them from church. They lowered the rock off the bed of the truck onto a heavy duty four-wheeled trolley. Roberta stood with her mother on the edge of the grass and marveled at the rock. It was just as she had imagined. The mass stood nearly three feet tall and measured nearly the same in width, though it was anything but symmetrical. The front of it had been hewed flat in a one foot by one foot section for the plaque, which wasn't ready yet. They started pulling the hand trolley off the pebbled driveway, but it quickly sank in the soggy spring grass. They would not be able to pull it as is. They borrowed planks from the back end of the Ares' shed and made wooden tracks which were used to pull the rock towards the pole sticking out of the ground.

At the moment Mr. Goodwin pulled the pole out, Roberta felt a knot in the pit of her stomach. It was silly, she thought. But without the pole there, it was like Trigger had been erased. *What if the rock wasn't on the exact spot?* Again, not a logical reflection since the rock was much larger than the tiny spot taken up by the pole. But still, at that moment, all proof of a grave had disappeared, and if everyone had walked away from the scene, Trigger would have been forgotten, much like Daddy, she thought. He didn't even have a pole, or so it seemed since her mother or grandmother never gave any information about his body. Her fear of Trigger's lost grave dissipated as the three men pushed the massive stone off the trolley over the spot of the long-standing pole. Trigger had his memorial marker.

"Johnson's engraving in town said that the plaque should be ready next week," he said.

"Thank you so much, Mr. Goodwin. We really appreciate it," said Roberta's mother.

"Where did you get the rock?" asked Roberta.

"Tom here," he pointed to one of the other men, "works in the quarry. He was able to get this nice chunk of limestone. He even sliced off the front to make a flat spot for the plaque. I think it's going to look nice."

"Thank you again."

The men stacked the planks behind the shed and left. Roberta stayed alone at the rock and climbed on top of it. She wasn't sure if Trigger would mind or not, finally concluding that he wouldn't. She could even stand on it, and when she did, she was tall enough to peek over the top of the shrubs on the front corner of the house and see the lake in the distance. She didn't know what this meant, but she thought it appropriate that when perched on top of Trigger's rock, she could see the place where she last saw him alive and where her daddy gave his goodbye speech. It felt perfect. Almost.

Perfection arrived a week later as Mr. Goodwin returned with the plaque. He used a hand-cranked drill for over half an hour to hollow out a place for anchors which would hold the plaque's screws in place. As he prepared the surface, Roberta read the plaque several times, marveling at the words she had created. She especially was delighted that a dog's paw print had been engraved into the bottom right corner.

"I thought that would be a nice touch," Mr. Goodwin added.

Roberta's mother agreed.

At long last, Mr. Goodwin inserted the screws through the pre-drilled holes on the plaque and attached it to the smooth surface of the rock. Then he stood back and paused for a moment.

"It's done."

Grandma and Mother looked in silence. The memories on their faces spoke their intent.

"Roberta, I'm really sorry about your dog. No one should ever have to lose a dog like that."

More meaning hung in the air. They all sensed it, but no one verbalized it any more. They would focus on the dog.

Roberta hugged Mr. Goodwin. She wasn't sure why. She had hugged Jed Travers. Why not Mr. Goodwin? He didn't mean to kill the dog, and he had done everything to make it right.

"Mrs. Ares. Ma'am." He nodded his head awkwardly at the ladies and gathered his tools to leave.

"Roberta, you're becoming a fine young lady," her grandmother said.

"Why do you say that?"

"What you did for Mr. Goodwin was very thoughtful."

"What did I do?"

"Well, you hugged him."

"I did? Oh."

Roberta's mother rested her hand on the top of the rock. "It's a beautiful memorial. A rock for you to play on and a place to remember Trigger. It's all very nice."

"Mom?"

"Yes?"

"What about Daddy?"

"What do you mean?"

"He still doesn't have a memorial."

"Roberta, we talked about this."

"Why can't we get another rock and put a plaque on it for Daddy."

"No, we're not doing that."

"Why not?"

"Roberta, we're finished talking about this." Her mother turned away and started walking towards the house.

"Mom, I want a plaque for Daddy!" Her voice had risen to an unladylike level. "I want a rock for Daddy!"

"Roberta, stop it."

"Why don't you want to remember Daddy?"

Her mother turned around and pointed her finger at her daughter.

"I will not go out of my house every day and stare at a rock that tells me my husband is never coming back. I know that already. And so do you, Roberta. No rock. No stone. No plaque. Your father is gone, and it's time for you to accept it and move on with your life."

"Tricia, do you need to be this harsh?" Grandma Newsom questioned.

"Yes, Mother, I do. We can't be mopping around here forever. We have lives to live. I miss my dear Daniel every day, but I've got work to do. Roberta has schoolwork she has to focus on. We have to build a future, and I can't continue running away crying every time I feel emotional. It's about time that we become strong. All of us. We have to. Roberta, am I clear?"

Roberta didn't respond. She stared at her mother—for once free of tears. She could tell her mother had no intention of running away. She wasn't going to excuse herself and cover her face with her hands. She looked different, but Roberta didn't know why. She did know her mother was wrong. She knew it with every fiber of her being. She would not forget. She couldn't. She still believed.

Chapter 14

The Row Boat

On April 29, 1945, Roberta celebrated her tenth birthday. Her mother and grandmother made a big deal out of it. Cousins stopped by after church, and they played in the back yard and ate cake.

Roberta's birthday wish was simple: "For the war to end." She almost added, "… so Daddy can come home," but she knew that it wouldn't be taken well. He was dead, they would say. He wasn't coming back, they would say. It would ruin her birthday, so she spoke in general terms, and everyone seemed pleased.

Her cousins hadn't seen Trigger's grave, and she proudly explained what happened.

"The truck ran over Trigger, and he laid on the side of the road with blood making the snow red."

She had a riveted audience, and for some reason, she didn't mind romanticizing the incident in such grotesque terms.

"And they put his body under this rock?"

"He was in a plain sack with blood dripping

from its bottom."

She said it with a spooky story quality that elicited the ohhhs and ahhhs and squeals from two female cousins not as strong as Roberta.

"A pole stuck out of the ground for many months. Only a pole. But I told my mom we needed a rock and a plaque. I wrote the words."

She displayed an air of pride. For all the hurt she had endured, this rock felt like the one thing she could depend on. Day in and day out she'd look out her bedroom window and the massive rock would still be there. Unmovable. Unlike people. Unlike the shifting moods of the water. A rock stays.

"And now Trigger's body is under this rock waiting for the day of the resurrection."

"Resurrection?"

"When all the bodies buried around the world will rise into the sky and meet Christ in the clouds!"

"That's not true," cousin Bobby protested.

"Yes, it is! Pastor Jenkins even said so."

"Not about dogs. Dog bodies don't resurrect."

"Yes they do."

"How's a dead body going to lift that rock off the ground?"

"It's magic, that's how."

The tale of the dog morphed into a near fistfight, which Grandma Newsom wisely broke up the brouhaha with a round of fresh lemonade.

By late afternoon, Roberta's mother called for the attention of the cousin crew from the back yard.

"Come here, everyone."

The five kids ran down the sloped backyard without question, no doubt hoping for another round of snacks.

"Go around front."

They did. As Roberta rounded the corner, she noticed Jed Travers standing in the middle of the sidewalk which led from the front door to the edge of the road.

"Hi, Roberta. Happy birthday!"

"Thanks."

"Jed came to see if …" her mother tried to explain then stopped. "Oh, Jed. Why don't you tell them?"

"Well, would anyone like to go on a boat ride? I brought my row boat."

A chorus of 'me's" rang through the air. Jed had rowed over from his house in town and pulled the boat ashore right at the edge of the park across the street.

"I could take two or three of you at a time. We could take turns rowing. And don't worry. It's completely safe. And if someone falls in, I'll be right there to catch them."

Everyone agreed and trudged to the edge of the water. The birthday girl boarded first, along with Bobby and his little sister, Andrea. This would be the first time Roberta had been on the water since the day of the accident. She felt a little funny climbing into the boat. Her eyes remained on the area of the lake which had swallowed her, almost halfway to the tree-lined shore on the other side. She wasn't exactly afraid. Jed was there, and she knew he would protect her. But she felt distant, like there was something left for her to do, but she didn't know what. Her father's image kept pulsing through her head—but only the images from the photos on the mantle. She tried to think hard about him, about his face the day he took her to the water, but she had difficulty seeing anything except the photos. This upset her, though she had no idea what to do about it.

Bobby and Roberta each took one of the oars. Jed sat behind them with Andrea at the bow.

"Row! Row!" Jed said whimsically.

They set out into the water and soon the apprehension in Roberta's chest fled. She sailed again on the open water, heading towards an unknown destination. She barely heard anything Jed or Bobby or Andrea said. She just rowed and kept her eyes on the progress. During a moment deep in thought, Jed signaled to turn around.

"Roberta. Roberta."

She broke from her trance.

"We need to turn back. Give the other kids a chance."

As he instructed them how to turn the boat around, Roberta asked him a question about his demeanor. "Why are you so happy today, Jed?"

"Well, the news says the war in Europe is almost over. Can you believe it? The Germans could surrender any day now."

"Does that mean all the soldiers would come home?" asked Roberta.

"Well, not likely. There's still the war going on against Japan. I imagine many of the soldiers would be heading over there."

"Let's pretend this is a war boat," said Bobby. "Fire." He made an explosion with his mouth. It took a moment for Roberta to join in, but she too sent imaginary shells exploding over the heads of the onlookers on shore.

Was the war really ending? What does that mean for daddy?

After the boat rides had ended, the women invited Jed for dessert with the family.

Dusk set in and a few distant thunderclaps warned of a coming storm. Roberta sat alone on the front steps for a moment staring out over the distant water. She couldn't shake the thought of the boat, and she knew she had no right to entertain the thought reoccurring in her mind, but this was her chance. For real. She would never get another. She sprung into action. She ran upstairs and grabbed her wooden airplane. Within seconds she was out the front door and crossing the street.

"Roberta. Hey, what are you doing?" Bobby yelled after her. She didn't stop. She ran towards the boat and immediately pushed it into the water. It wasn't as easy as she thought. The back was stuck on the edge of a rock, and she had to finagle it off until it started floating on its own.

"Roberta, what are you doing?"

She stopped for a moment and looked back at her cousin.

"Leave me be, Bobby. I'm going out on the water."

"You're not allowed."

"You're not my mother."

"I'm going to tell your mother."

"Go ahead, you tattle-tale."

"Roberta, you can't take the boat out by yourself."

"No one believes me, and I'm going to prove them wrong."

"Believes you about what?"

"I'm going across the lake, Bobby. And you can't stop me."

"Roberta."

She pushed hard and the boat's bow drifted free in the edge of the water. She jumped head first into the boat.

"I'm going to tell!"

"I don't care."

Bobby ran off. She struggled at first to turn the boat around. Earlier she only had to contend with one oar, and the cumbersome task made her think she would never leave the shore. She had placed the airplane propped up on the seat in the bow, and she glanced at it once out of frustration.

"Come on, fly!"

She pushed off with both oars and maneuvered the row boat in the correct direction.

"Attack!" She wasn't sure why she used military terms, but she paced herself and got better at rhythmic rowing. She glanced back once, not to notice if anyone followed her, but to see the ominous sky trail overhead with a message of uncertainty. A crack of thunder and a bolt shot across the sky horizontally. *Heat lighting,* she said to herself. *Go, just go. Ride the storm. War is storm. Onward.* She encouraged herself with every row of the oar.

The water became choppier as she moved towards the center of the lake—her arms tiring. The airplane flipped backwards off the edge of the bow seat and lay at her feet. She couldn't stop to pick it up, but continued on, eyes set on the shore approaching her but always still a long way off.

She felt the first drop of rain right about the time she arrived at the location of the thin ice which sucked her underneath. The child shook-off fears of falling or failing, and stroked forward even harder. Her forearms burnt, but the upside down airplane at her feet encouraged her onward. Each row a further cry for her father: *I'm coming. I will see the other side. I will not forget you even if everyone else does. Even if Mother has.*

The sky darkened like a melodic symphony being snuffed out by a black blanket, leaving only short expressive melodic tones to remain in her heart. The drop multiplied to a sprinkle. The water tipped and tottered in the open, splashing loudly off the sides of the boat. The wind whirled around the girl like an Old Testament prophet being sucked into the sky by a greater unknown purpose. The fear, in-planted within her, sprouted. Not without cause. She remembered the deep of the water very well, and she didn't want to experience it again. She looked in each direction and saw no one else in the encroaching darkness. *Where would her angel come from? How would Jed Travers find her out here?* She had his boat. *Foolish.* For a moment that's how she felt. She heard the harsh words from her mother: *Roberta, why would you do this?* She knew why but couldn't explain it to anyone else. Not in a way they would understand. She knew that death was final and that there was no war on the other side of this lake, but on the day her daddy had spoken to her, it sounded so convincing, like if she followed far enough the magic would allow the desires of her heart to be fulfilled.

But fear gripped her, and she decided to turn around. Or at least try. She stood up, leaning her calves against the back of the seat, and used both arms to push off with the right oar to create a circular motion with the boat. As she struggled against the ever-moving water, a thunderous clap cracked overheard. The kind that jolts the life out of one's heart for a second and sends a person's stomach into the pit of the unknown. She yelled and tripped backwards on the seat, catching her foot underneath. As she tried to straighten herself, she leaned sideways and slid over the side of the boat into the water. The coldness consumed her, not like the last time—there were no shards of ice—but the stark shock to her system made her breathe in a mouthful of water as she slid underneath. Seconds was what she had. She looked for the white-winged creature, but the darkened surface offered no such help. Only a long object floating above her—the boat, with the oar still flapping up and down on the water. She closed her eyes and straightened out her arms. She could see the white descending towards her. Two large wings spread out over her. A head not visible but a translucent way forward. *Rise,* she thought. *Rise and search. Rise and live. Rise.* Her father's face emerged in her mind—not from the photographs—but from the shore of the lake when she sat on his lap, and they played with the butterfly. He surrounded her, as did the wings, the white frightening wings that buoyed her on. She gasped over the surface of the water and realized her arms were clinging to the oar still connected to the rowing station. Rain poured like solid sheets, pounding her in the face and making even an attempt to yell out into the evening sky futile. She clung onto the oar like an infant coddled under the arms of its mother.

"You can do it, Roberta."

She heard the voice. Maybe audible. Maybe in her head. The familiar voice encouraged her on. "You can do it."

She let go with her right arm and gripped it

higher up on the oar. With a violent heave, through the unrelenting stings on her face, she surged upward and plopped headfirst into the row boat, unsure of exactly how she did it. As she opened her eyes, she was face-to-face with the airplane, now in a small puddle of water like it had been crashed into its own sea.

"Go home."

She said this to herself, or heard herself think it, or heard another voice say it to her. She didn't think of the distant shore and the tips of the trees, which were no longer visible. She thought of home. She pushed onward, not knowing exactly where to go, but she struggled through the exhaustion, through the weather, through her fears, because she put her fears behind her. Row after row, push after push, through mangled thoughts and desperate coldness she heard the voice again. More than one. Coming through the rain. She pushed again, and as if a veil had been lifted, she saw them, all of them, standing frantically on the shore yelling and screaming one name: Roberta.

She smiled and rowed harder and the screams grew in elation as they recognized the desperate child coming home once again. No one displayed anger when she arrived, when Jed Travers waded out to his shoulders to help guide the boat back the rest of the way. She screamed for her mother and jumped out of the boat and into her arms, her mother's knees saddled into the dirt, Sunday dress soaked, hair matted like a frightened cat left outside in a storm. She cried on her mother's shoulder. That was all she wanted to do. That was all she needed to do, and the birthday was complete. She turned ten but perhaps grew much older than one more candle on this particular day.

Chapter 15

V-E Day

Her mother never inquired about the reason Roberta took the boat on her own. The distress in the little girl's mind resonated beyond any lecture or scolding she needed to hear. She had made a mistake, and, for that matter, it was doubtful she would ever do it again.

Roberta, however, wanted to discuss it but not with her mother or grandmother. She asked for Jed Travers. Mrs. Ares telephoned him one evening and asked if he wouldn't mind stopping by to talk with Roberta. He sat on the living room sofa with Roberta positioned across from him in her favorite armed swivel chair. She held the airplane in her hand.

"I heard you found the airplane. That's really great. It's remarkable, really, that it would float back to shore right where you found it."

Roberta nodded at his thought then turned to her mother. "Mom, can I speak with Jed alone for a moment?"

"Oh, well, sure. I'll be in the kitchen if you need me."

"I won't."

"What if Jed wants a snack?"

"He won't."

"Unless you have any of that pie left, Mrs. Ares."

Roberta scowled at him. *He must not set the agenda. This is my time,* she thought.

"Never mind about the pie."

"I'll have it for you when you're finished talking."

"Thank you, Mrs.—"

"Mom. Please allow us to have our meeting."

"Sorry."

Jed shifted uncomfortably in his seat as if sitting in front of a school principal—a miniature one with folded arms and commanding authority.

"Roberta, how can I help you?"

"Do you believe in angels?"

"Angels? Well, I guess I do. I've heard Pastor Jenkins preach about them a time or two. He wouldn't steer us wrong."

"What do you think they look like?"

"I hadn't really thought about it. Wings, I guess. I guess I picture angels in white robes, but I'm not really sure. Why?"

"Do you think angels live in water? Or can swim underwater?"

"Roberta, I'm really not an expert on angels …"

"Do you think we each have a guardian angel?"

"Well, I don't know. I suppose—"

"Have you ever seen your guardian angel?"

"Well, no … I …"

"Are you my guardian angel? Are you really Jed Travers?"

Jed didn't reply this time. His face stared back at her like an unpainted side of a barn. Roberta watched him intently as he squirmed back and forth on the sofa. Eventually, Jed tried to break through the silence.

"Roberta—"

She didn't let him. She pressed.

"Are you Jed Travers?"

"Of course! That's my name."

"Who were your parents?"

"Samuel and Jane Travers. I'm pretty sure you've seen them at church."

"And you don't have wings?"

"Roberta!"

"Can you swim underwater without breathing?"

"Roberta, what are you trying to ask?"

"And you're sure angels exist, but you aren't one?"

"Yes, I believe that angels exist, and I know for sure that I am not one."

"Fine. You may now go eat your pie."

Roberta stood up and walked toward the staircase, but Jed spoke up.

"No, no, no. You called me over here … Roberta, sit down."

Surprisingly, she obeyed, curious as to what crossed the mind of the non-angel. "You called me here to talk, and you asked me strange questions about angels. What's this all about?"

"I'll do the asking."

"No you won't. I will ask too. What's this about?"

Should she tell him? She asked herself and leaned back in the chair. She pushed with her foot until the swivel chair turned her back towards him. She needed a moment on her own. She stared into the dining room and heard her mother rummaging around in the kitchen.

"Roberta?"

He kept the pressure on her.

"Why did you want to talk to me? If you have spiritual questions about angels, perhaps you should ask Pastor Jenkins."

She twirled around in the chair until she faced him directly.

"I don't want to ask Pastor Jenkins. I want to

ask you. You must be an angel." Her voice yearned with passion. Almost a pleading. She wanted it to be true.

"Roberta, why are you asking me this?"

She lowered her head and spoke in monotone. "When I fell out of the row boat, I saw the white wings. The same white wings that saved me when I fell through the ice. But this time, you weren't in the rowboat. Were you?"

He didn't answer.

"I opened my eyes under the water and two wings had covered me and at that moment I knew what to do to get back to the surface and climb into the boat."

"Oh … wow … Roberta …"

"Jed?"

"Yes?"

"Do you think my daddy is an angel?"

A long pause passed between them. She knew what she wanted him to answer, but she also knew he wouldn't say it. He couldn't. How would he know? Even though he saved her once.

"Roberta, I do believe your daddy is watching over you."

That's all she needed to hear. She nodded at him and stood up. "Mom, Jed wants his pie."

"I didn't say that."

"It's ready for him," she called from the

kitchen.

Roberta walked up the stairs and into her room. She sat on the bench by her window and looked out into the backyard splashed with evening shadows, but she could still see the rock. It commanded her attention. For the first time, she wondered if it was better for her father not to have a rock of his own. Not to have a plaque of his own. Does that allow him to be free? To roam around the world and look after her? Did it allow him to swoop beneath the surface of the water and encourage her on to safety? She didn't know the answers to anything except this: she missed him.

***

May 8, 1945

Roberta's war-torn town briefly sprung to life on May 8. Even though the town didn't have any physical holes from exploding German artillery, or its houses weren't riddled with pock marks from the mounted machine gun of a swooping Japanese fighter, the town was as war-torn and war-weary as any little village in the French countryside. When the early morning edition of the newspaper boasted the best news possible—

VICTORY IN EUROPE—everyone took the joy to the streets in a spontaneous burst of jubilation.

Grandma Newsom read the account first and yelled throughout the house. Morning had broken, and the sun had burst through for the first time, not only on the sleeping town but also on the weary souls.

"Roberta, Tricia!"

She held the paper over her head with both arms as the mother and daughter joyfully looked on from the landing halfway up the staircase. Horns beeped as they went by heading to town. There was not a moment to lose. "Get dressed. I'll get the car ready."

When Roberta ran to the car in the driveway, she noticed the back window rolled down and a large flag pole holding the stars and stripes protruding and draping down over the door.

"Roberta. Hold it high and proud."

She would. She slid in from the other door and grasped the flag pole in her hands. She lifted it up straight above the car with the pole itself still resting against the inside of the door.

"You hold Old Glory tight," Grandma said.

"I will, Grandma. I will."

Roberta stuck her head out the window and watched the stripes in a mesmerizing back and forth pattern, with the rapid fire *tooow, tooow,*

tooow sound from the wind flapping through the air.

The entire town formed an impromptu parade which circled endlessly around the Civil War Memorial Park at the roundabout in front of the county courthouse. Flags, like sparklers, caught the morning sun from the crowds swarming on the sidewalks and spreading small glints of red, white, and blue with every flap. An elderly gentleman clung onto the side of the war memorial and blasted his trumpet. A revelry of renewal. The local drum and fife group, affiliated with the survivors of the WWI association, showed up in full force and marched in the traffic alongside the slow-moving cars honking incessantly.

Bridger's Bakery set up a table in front of the courthouse and handed out free donuts slapped with red, white, and blue icing. They didn't last long in the swarm. Members of the Methodist church, opposite the courthouse, knelt on the steps and prayed a prayer of thanksgiving to God. A group of mothers, whose boys had gone off to war, hugged each other in a never-ending scrum next to the war memorial with its granite obelisk pointed to heaven.

The immersive scene entranced Roberta—the sounds, tears, and exuberance not seen in this town for far too long. Everyone belonged in the moment, as if they too were the soldiers finally able to rest on the weary edge of the battlefield. Roberta had never seen anything like it, and it enthralled her, until she saw the tears coming down her mother's cheek. She kept wiping them, but they were there. Obvious. With the war being over, a new phase began. But what? What does it all mean? *Do soldiers come home? What about the ones who can't come home? What about Daddy?* Thoughts overran her, like the paper-clenching townsfolk who swarmed the war memorial.

Grandma Newsom circled her car in the chaos several times until she veered off the roundabout and parked on a side street. The three of them walked through the throngs, greeting people, and yelling as loud as the next one.

At 9 AM, the church bells from both the Methodist church and the Catholic church down Third Avenue sounded on cue. But the bells didn't mark the time of day or even the sentiment of the moment. The bells tolled for a purpose more ominous—a blatant reminder of the planned memorial service for nineteen-year-old Malty Manyard.

Of all the men from Roberta's hometown who lost their lives in the great war, Malty was the youngest. The tragedy had been announced a week before with the planned memorial on May 8. When the bells sounded, the jubilation turned introspective, and the entire town walked the side street to the Catholic church, the largest place in town to hold a service. The bells had sucked the joy from the atmosphere as a solemn reminder of why they were so happy. The end of death. The end of destruction. The end of unanswered questions and sleepless nights.

The opening prayer alternated between thanksgiving for the end of the European war and sorrow for the one who would "serve us malts over at Pete's Parlor." It's how he got his nickname: Malty.

Roberta sat on her mother's lap. There weren't enough seats for everyone. She thought about Malty. She knew him. He was only nine years older than her. She remembered how he would place the ice cream sundaes down in front of her. One time she asked for extra whipped cream, and he brought over a large bowl of the fluffy white stuff stacked so high on top of her sundae that the top slid off right onto Roberta's sleeve. Malty apologized, but Roberta laughed and licked her sleeve with her mouth until it was free of whipped cream and until her mother scolded her for her ill manners. That was the boy. She remembered him. He didn't look like a soldier.

He wore a white apron and a white soda jerk cap. And now he was dead.

"We wish to remember Franklin 'Malty' ..."

Dead. *What did it mean? Was he killed by a bullet? Was he in a plane like Daddy? Did it hurt? Did he see white wings to protect and help him? And if not, why not? Didn't he have a guardian angel? Why did he have to die? Can he now talk with Daddy in heaven?* Constant thoughts flooded her mind.

As the service ended, they waited in line for thirty minutes to pay their respects to Malty's family at the front of the church. Roberta didn't speak. Again, there was no body. Nothing to see. No coffin. No bloody sack.

As the three of them exited the church, a man and a woman, in their Sunday-best clothes, greeted Roberta's mother with a calm enthusiasm.

"This is my mother," said Mrs. Ares, pointing to Grandma Newsom.

Grandma shook both of their hands.

"I believe I had met your husband a few times at the Rod and Gun Club," said the man. Roberta supposed he was older than Mother yet younger than Grandma, though she couldn't be sure.

"That sounds right. He would go there on occasion."

Mrs. Ares then pointed to Roberta. "And this

is my daughter, Roberta."

"It's a pleasure to meet you," said the woman, holding out her hand to shake.

Her mother nudged her, and Roberta offered her hand in greeting.

"How old are you?"

"Ten."

"What a wonderful age."

"Roberta, this is Mr. & Mrs. Warner. I don't know if you remember, but your father's friend used to come over and visit sometimes. He worked with your daddy. These are his parents. He was a very good friend of your father."

"Is he in the war too?"

"Yes," Mr. Warner replied. "He went the same time as your father."

"Did he die too?"

The bluntness of the question caught everyone off guard.

"Ah, no. Paul is alive. We're very sorry about the loss of your father. He was such a good man."

"I know. So Paul didn't have a bad eye?" Everyone looked at her strangely. "I want to go home," she said.

Her grandmother took her hand, and they walked towards the car a few blocks away. She looked back and watched as her mother talked with the couple in a friendly way.

"Grandma?"

"Yes."

"Why do some people die in war, but others don't?"

Her grandma didn't answer. She just patted Roberta's hand, and they waited in the car for her mother to return.

Chapter 16

The 4th of July

Roberta raced down the stairs on the bright morning of July 4th. She dreamed of this day—the town picnic by the lake, the return of the beauty pageants and the soap box auto races. She would be there for it all. In the evening she would run through the darkness with her neighborhood friends, lighting sparklers and throwing them into the tree branches.

"Mom!"

The house seemed empty, but both the front and back doors were swung open wide to allow the warm summer breeze to seep through the screen doors.

She called again but no answer. She ran into the kitchen and glanced out the back door. She caught a glimpse of Trigger's rock but not her mother. As she was ready to run through the house and look out front, she noticed a shoe box sitting on the kitchen table. It contained many envelopes ripped open at the top. A few of them lay plainly on the tabletop. All were addressed to Tricia Ares. One letter exposed itself to whoever walked by. It happened to be Roberta. She sat down in front of it in the chair which had already been pulled out from the table, and she took the letter in her hands and started reading.

Dear Tricia,

Who was writing? She glanced at the bottom.

Love, Paul

Her eyes swung upward again, and she started reading the first line.

I received your last letter and it made me quite content. I think of you every day, and it makes the danger around me seem distant. I have a purpose when I think about you.

Roberta stopped reading and raised her head in puzzlement. Paul. Who's Paul? She turned over the envelope and read the return address. There were all kinds of numbers and letters on it including A.P.O. It had been postmarked New York, NY. *Who is Paul in New York,* she thought. *And why is New York so dangerous? And why does he say love?*

She looked at the three other envelopes on the table. They all had the same return address. Paul

Warner. Lots of numbers and letters. A.P.O. New York, NY. She flipped through the envelopes in the shoe box. The same. She glanced back at the letter.

The photo you sent of yourself is lovely. You are so beautiful. I keep it on me at all times. It is my good luck charm. I know that it keeps me safe, and one day I'll be able to see you face to face. I hope it is not forward of me to say that I wish to hold your hand and even kiss you. I know I've said too much, but in a place like this, thoughts such as these make the passing time bearable.

Roberta had to look once again at the front of the envelope to make sure. It said Tricia Ares. She knew her mother's name was Tricia, and the letters were sitting on Tricia Ares' kitchen table. But she couldn't make sense of them. *Kiss? Who is he talking to? Kiss. He wants to kiss Tricia? Why? Who is Paul Warner?*

As myriad thoughts overwhelmed Roberta, the front screen door slammed shut and footsteps patted towards her. She didn't move or flinch at all. She looked back over her shoulder and caught her mother frozen mid-step, glaring at her child sitting in front of the letters. Her mother lunged forward and grabbed one out of Roberta's hand, scooping up the shoe box and stuffing the loose envelopes inside.

"Roberta, those aren't for you!"

"They were left open on the table."

"I was just chasing away some rabbits from the garden and … you didn't read any of them, did you?"

Roberta paused. She wasn't supposed to read the letters. *Why? Because of the kiss?*

"Who is Paul, and why does he want to kiss you?"

"Roberta. These are private. These are not for you."

"Who is Paul?"

"Roberta!"

"Mom! Who is Paul, and why does he want to kiss you?"

Roberta's grandmother came into view behind her mother. "Tricia, you should tell her."

"It's my life. My private life!" yelled her mother.

"Not anymore. Tell your daughter."

"Mom!" Roberta stared straight upward into her mother's face.

"Roberta, sit down!"

"Why does Paul want to kiss you? Why do you have so many letters from Paul? Who's Paul?"

"Tricia, please. Just talk to Roberta."

Her mother wavered between crying and yelling. Her eyes had welled up but had yet to release anything upon her cheek. She slammed the shoe box on the table and pointed for Roberta to sit herself back down.

"Tricia, it's not the girl's fault. She didn't do anything wrong."

A forced smile came over her mother's face. "Yes, you're right. Sorry, Roberta. You didn't do anything wrong. I left the letters out. Sorry."

"Who's Paul?"

Her grandmother sat on the other side of her, across from her mother. "Do you remember on V-E Day, after we left church, we met a man and woman?"

Roberta nodded.

"Those are Paul's parents. I've known their family for a long time. Your father and I were both good friends with Paul when we were young. We went to school together. Paul was your father's best friend. They did pilot training together and eventually went off to war together."

Roberta acknowledged the information. She was about to ask again when her mother continued.

"After your father's death, last December, Paul was kind enough to write to me. He loved your father dearly, like a brother. So it was hard for him too. We wrote to comfort each other in ways that adults can do with one another. I don't expect you to understand, but Paul has been very helpful to me in dealing with your father's death. So we are good friends who help each other."

Roberta pondered the explanation. *Good friends. Help each other. Like a brother.* She still had a question.

"Why does he want to kiss you?"

Her mother looked over to Grandma, who said nothing. But she had a look about her and nudged her on.

"Roberta … Paul means a lot to me."

"Doesn't Daddy mean a lot to you?"

"Roberta, of course. I love your Daddy with all my heart and always will."

"Then why does Paul want to kiss you?"

"Roberta, please."

"Mom!"

"Your father is dead! Paul and I have expressed our love for each other. Now, I'm sorry. This isn't the way I wanted to tell you, but please try and understand."

Roberta stood up abruptly from the table. The back of the chair flipped over onto the floor.

"I don't want Paul. I want Daddy."

"Nobody is replacing your Daddy."

"Why do you want to kiss another man?"

"Because your father is dead. And I have to live." The tears came down Tricia's cheeks.

Then Roberta said it: "I hope Paul dies too. Just like Daddy!"

She ran out of the room and up the staircase. She jumped onto her bed and buried her head into the pillow. She thought of a strange man, all the men she knew, kissing her mother. She didn't know what Paul looked like, but she did know Mr. Goodwin. Would he kiss her? She thought of her mother doing so. It made her scream. Then the image of Jed Travers kissing her mother flashed through her mind. Then Mr. Warner—the man from the church kissing her. Then the weirdest of all, she thought of Pastor Jenkins kissing her mother. It made her angry. She yelled into the pillow and pounded her fist on the mattress as hard as she could. No one came to stop her, not even Grandma. She screamed and hit the bed until her eyes closed and she fell back asleep from exhaustion.

***

Roberta emerged from her room a couple of hours later. She had spent the time thinking, drawing, staring at the rock in the backyard, feeling angry at her mother, but it all went away as she heard the car pull out of the driveway. She thought she had been left alone on one of her favorite holidays. She raced downstairs to see Grandma sitting at the kitchen table.

"Where did Mom go?"

"She went to the celebration at the lake."

"She left without me?"

"You didn't seem to want to go."

"I do!"

"All right. All right. I thought so. Mrs. Wilkins is going in a bit. I'll phone her and ask if we can go with her." She stood up and patted Roberta on the head. "You shouldn't be so hard on your mother. She's trying to do the right thing, you know. She loves you dearly. More than anything."

"More than she loves Paul."

"Roberta, stop that. Paul is her friend. She needs an adult friend who understands her needs too. It doesn't mean she loves you less. Nothing could."

They went to the park by the lake, and Roberta spent the afternoon running around in complete bliss. She even ran into her mother a couple times without incident, including the ride home in the car all together.

But Roberta wasn't about to let it go. She

couldn't. The stack of letters piled up in her mind.

"Mom, did Daddy send you letters from the war?"

"Yes, of course."

"Did you keep them?"

"Yes, of course I did. They are precious to me."

"Did he ask you for a kiss in them?"

"Roberta, stop that."

She wouldn't.

As tradition had it, Patty's house, which was one door over across the empty lot, had invited the Ares family to the July 4th evening bonfire. The kids would run around with sparklers and grill hot dogs on sticks over the fire, while the adults would sit around and socialize.

Roberta charred two hot dogs to perfection and ate them both as the evening sky grew dark. The fire flickered lights on the happy faces. She had mixed feelings about the happiness. On the one hand it made her forget everything and the sweat of running in the humid air felt freeing to her. She felt alive. On the other hand, the smile on her mother's face irritated her. *Why was she so happy? Was it because of Paul? Or the end of the war? Or …* and then they arrived. That couple from the church. The Warners. Patty's parents explained how they knew each other, a business connection

… "and I knew that the Warners were friends with the Ares, so I invited them over."

Patty's father brought two wicker rockers from the back porch, and Mr. & Mrs. Warner joined the revelry. They said hello to Roberta, but as soon as they did, she ran off to play with the others; however, she never stopped watching them. They seemed so happy, and so did her mother who sat beside them. Tricia Ares looked at home, gabbing and laughing and being comfortable with the Warners. Too comfortable. Roberta fumed. She felt like an outsider, like she was losing her mother, and all of Grandmother's assurances weren't enough. Even if they were true, it didn't matter. She wanted to hurt her mother. She wanted to hurt the Warners. Then she thought of the way.

She ran past the bonfire and spoke to her grandmother in passing.

"Grandma, I'm going to the house. Be right back."

"All right, dear."

She ran across the empty lot between their two houses and through the back screen door. She ran through the kitchen and living room, up the stairs, flipping on the light switch first, and into the second bedroom on the right—her mother's room. She opened the closet door and first looked up, then on the floor. She found it. The shoebox. She bent over and lifted the lid just to make sure. Letters. She put the lid back on and tucked the box under her arm. Down the steps, out the door, across the lawn. She came to an abrupt halt at the fire, at the opposite end of her mother.

"Roberta?" her mother inquired.

Roberta lifted the box into the air, removed the lid and dumped the letters onto the bonfire.

"There! There! There!" she yelled.

Roberta's mother stood up in shock. "Roberta!"

"There!"

"Roberta, no!"

"There!"

"Roberta! Those are your father's letters! No!"

The words rung in her ears. Your father's letters. She looked into the fire. The flames devoured each word, each sheet, each postage stamp, each *Love, Daniel*. She refused to believe it for a moment. These were the letters from the shoe box. But when she saw the horror on her mother's face, the sickness delved into the pit of her stomach. There was nothing she could do to take it back. All the words, all the final words from her father, all the tender thoughts and the veiled fear. All gone, disintegrated into wisps of gray smoke. All the phrases: "Please tell Roberta

I love her" were absorbed into the atmosphere forever tinged by the roaring heat of the fire. Roberta put her hands on her head. The tears poured. She screamed in agony. She screamed in fear. She screamed that she was alone and now even the piece of her father she had known disappeared forever. She felt distant from her mother. There was no one but her. She collapsed onto the ground behind the fire. Both her grandmother and mother ran to her and held her in their arms. The whole evening fell quiet, except for the crackling fire. No one spoke a word, allowing the flames to flicker on the unspeakable loss everyone felt.

***

As Roberta lay in bed later in the evening, replaying the events in her head, her mother walked in carrying a shoe box. She placed it at the foot of Roberta's bed.

"Here they are. If you want to burn them, burn them."

Roberta didn't respond.

"They are just words on paper. It doesn't change the meaning in our hearts."

Roberta wanted to say she was sorry, but the words wouldn't come.

"Burn them," her mother insisted.

Roberta looked away.

"I am very angry with you, Roberta. But I also know you are hurting. You miss your father, as you should, and I know you were acting out to remember him. But we will always remember him. How could we not? You are his child. That will never change. I'm sorry if you don't like the fact that Paul and I write to each other. But that's life. You have to live with things you don't like. But if it makes you feel better, go ahead and burn them."

She pushed the box closer to her.

"It's all right. My heart knows what they say, just as your heart knows how much your father will always love you."

Her mother turned around and walked out of the room. Roberta stared at the shoe box at her feet. She crawled out of the covers and picked up the box. She walked across the hall and placed it at the foot of her mother's bed. Then she returned to her own bed and fell asleep.

Chapter 17

The Cold War & the Big Bomb

Every day, Roberta stared at the photos of her daddy around the house. There were four of them. One of him in his uniform on the mantle. Another of his wedding day with his bride. One of him in a boat on the lake, fishing pole in his hand as he held up a large bass. And one of him and her mother with Roberta at age six standing between them. It was from the county fair, and she held cotton candy in her hands. Daddy had a big smile across his face. Most of her memories had morphed into these photos, and besides the important day with Trigger and the butterfly at the lake, she had fewer and fewer memories of her father.

The photo with the uniform had become especially troubling. She often thought of taking the eraser end of her pencil and scratching out her father's face and drawing a new face instead. The illusive face from her mother's letters.

"Why do you want to replace Daddy?"

"Roberta, stop talking like that."

"Do you love Paul?"

"Roberta!"

Sometimes she held the eraser in her hands and lightly rubbed it on the glass, leaving behind splinters of red rubber on the glossy frame.

Certain days Roberta would get along with her mother just fine as if nothing had changed — as if they still waited for Daddy to return.

But other days Roberta would sit in silence and not speak to her mother, relying on Grandma for all the necessities of the day. Grandma didn't like it, and she told her so.

"Roberta, talk to your mother."
"Roberta, that's no way to treat your mother."

"But Mom has someone else to talk to."
"That's no way to treat Daddy!"

The on-again, off-again cold war took its toll on everybody. Roberta felt guilty about the burned letters but continued to keep an eye out for the arrival of new letters. Roberta and her mother played a game waiting for the mail — Roberta in hopes of intercepting an overseas correspondence — her mother in hopes of hiding the correspondence from the brooding youth.

On August first, the mailman came early on a Saturday while her mother was at the grocery store. A letter. She tucked it under her shirt and ran around the backside of the shed, stopping at Trigger's rock. She leaned against it, facing away from the house, and ripped open the letter. She would read it. All of it.

My Dearest Tricia,
I will be shipping out to the Pacific soon. My tasks here in Europe are over. The war is still raging, and I loathe to think how long it will be until I return home.

Loathe? She didn't understand. She poked her head up from behind the rock and peered into the kitchen. Her voice carried through the screen door to her grandma milling around at the counter.

"Grandma! Grandma!"

"Yes?" from the screen door.

"What does loathe mean?"

"Loathe? It means hate."

"Oh." She immediately plopped back down behind the rock.

I loathe to think … I hate to think. Roberta reread and thought to herself. Hmmm. *He will be gone a long time. A very long time. The Pacific. Is he going to fight Japan? Maybe his plane will crash. Maybe he'll never return,* she thought.

There's a question in my mind that I will one day ask. It's all I think about. One day we will be face to face, and you can be sure what I feel. Your words keep me alive.

Your words keep me alive. She repeated it again and again. Her words keep him alive. *Why didn't her words keep Daddy alive? Didn't she write to him?* Her thoughts circled her mind. Alive. Keep. Face to face. Her mind became absorbed in the words on the page that she didn't even hear the car pull up the driveway, but the slam of the door jolted her consciousness into the backyard. She poked her head up like a frightened groundhog and made a sound—like an ahhh—a surprise—and she bolted towards her burrow, letter in hand, yelling a quick "Hi Mom," in the process.

"Help me with the groceries!"

She barely heard that plea, and by the time her mind understood what her mother wanted, she had already run through the kitchen and was heading up the stairs.

"Roberta!"

A piece of paper had fallen from her grasp and lay in the grass near the walk to the back porch. Her mother held it in her hand and yelled upward through the open window to Roberta's room.

"Roberta! You opened my letter! Roberta!"

The girl looked down. Indeed. She only had the contents but not the envelope. Her heart burned with fear, and she sat passively as the raging sound from her mother inched closer, and the plodding, purposeful feet approached without hindrance. Her mother exploded through the door with the anger of the northern wind and whisked the contents of the letter from Roberta's hand before she could even respond.

"You evil child! You stole my letter. I've told you before that this is my business, not yours. You have no right to go snooping into an adult's business. I've had enough of your behavior. Your father's dead. He's dead!"

"No!" Roberta screamed. "I hate him. I hate Paul. I hate him. I hate you. I hate Daddy. No!"

"You're a selfish, selfish child! Can't you see I'm hurting too?! Can't you see what this has done to me?"

Both of them had tears streaming down, and Roberta saw something for the first time. She saw the pain in her heart written on her mother's face. It was like looking into a mirror. The loud words echoed her own.

"And don't you ever say that you hate your father. There's no one like him. No one who loved you more. No one else who would have done anything for you. Don't you see? He went to war for you. For you! So you can live your best life in the America that he loved. Can't you see it? I understand it hurts, but we can't continue like this. We have to move on. We have to."

Roberta noticed her grandmother at the door frame. She didn't say anything. She allowed the emotional heavyweight fighters to sting and jab until a resolution could be reached.

"I'm sorry. I'm sorry, Mom." A long pause passed between them. "Paul is going to the Pacific."

At that, her mother broke down in more tears and left the room. Roberta sat on the edge of her bed and stared out the window. Her grandmother slid in next to her on the bench. She patted Roberta's hand.

"This is hard, I know. One day, Roberta, all of this will make you stronger."

"I don't feel stronger."

"Not yet. But you will. I promise. Please don't take your mother's letters again."

"I won't."

"You should go tell her you love her." Roberta looked up at her grandma with a hint of surprise. "You do, you know. You love your mother very much. That's why you're so upset. And I always say, if you have to get upset, it might as well be because of love."

***

The war had cooled. At least in the house. Roberta lay flat on the living room floor with her doll and airplane in her grasp. She played quietly with the hum of the radio in the background. Her grandma sat knitting, and her mother held the newspaper in her hand and shifted back and forth on the swivel chair. An announcement was imminent from President Truman. Everyone stopped what they were doing and listened.

Truman spoke: "Sixteen hours ago an American airplane dropped one bomb on Hiroshima and destroyed its usefulness to the enemy. That bomb had more power than 20,000 tons of TNT …"

"Mom, what does that mean?"

"Shhhh … listen."

Truman continued: "It's an atomic bomb …"

Atomic bomb? Roberta questioned. Atomic. It didn't mean anything to her, but it sounded horrible. President Truman said many things, and the words glossed over her mind as she wondered why it all sounded so important. Grandma's and mother's faces showed concern but also a calm hope, a strange combination which hindered Roberta's understanding of the situation.

"What's an atomic bomb?"

"Shhhh—listen."

She spent the evening peppering her mother with questions about the bomb without ever hearing a satisfactory answer.

The next morning, the newspaper headline read: *Atomic Bomb Hits Japan!*

"How horrible!" she heard her mother say while reading the details.

"But isn't Japan our enemy?"

"Yes, but any bomb is horrible."

"Do you think Paul was there?"

"Roberta!"

Three days later. Another headline: *Atomic Bomb on 2nd Japanese City!*

Then it was over. The long war. The worry. The tears. The dead bodies without coffins. The church memorials without bodies.

August 15, 1945 headline: *V-J! The War is Over!*

The town exploded once more with jubilant celebrations. The three members of the Ares household drove to the center of town and parked on the side street. They didn't circle the monument and beep their horns like they did in May. They were more subdued. Tears, for sure.

Smiles abundant. But there was an emptiness in their walk, as if they entered the unknown, knowing that postwar life would never return to prewar normal.

Roberta thought of her father, and wondered if it was really true that he now wouldn't come home. She had been assured many times that her father was dead, and she cried many tears on numerous nights while thinking of that fact, but with no body, no coffin, no burial plot, no stone marker, and a still-raging war, it didn't feel real. The yelling and champagne and hollering seemed a distant cry for help, far more distant than the other side of the lake. With the war over, she knew she had to figure out what it really meant to live without her daddy.

Chapter 18

The Wrong Uniform

The last day of summer slipped away into the coolness of the evening. The front door remained open, and the screen door still hung in place, not willing to cede to the harshness of the on-coming season. Roberta sat on the sofa, flipping through the pages of her school reader, *Friends Far and Near,* when she heard a car stop out front. She turned and sunk her knees into the cushions of the sofa and looked out the picture window. What she saw made her heart pound fast, like she had fallen through the ice or slipped overboard into the surly water.

A man in a uniform stepped out of the car and made his way up the sidewalk towards the house. She froze for a moment, not willing to believe it, but knowing all along that she had to be right. This was the only possible outcome acceptable to her universe on any level.

"I knew it," she said out loud.

Grandma and Mother had been talking in the kitchen. They didn't hear the car stop.

"I knew it."

She jumped off the sofa and sprang to the screen door to watch the uniform approach. She hadn't even looked at his face. The uniform commanded her attention.

"I knew it."

The shiny wings on the left breast. The visor on the cap. The neatly pressed trousers and black reflective shoes polished to a shiny veneer.

She readied herself, her hopes had sprung. She would jump into his arms. She would cry and laugh at the wasted moments when she fought with her mother over this exact outcome.

She readied a scream of jubilation surpassing V-E and V-J days combined, until she finally looked at his face. It was not the same as the one in the frame on the mantle, nor the same as the one in her mind by the lake. She vacillated in her thoughts—part anger, part sorrow. It felt like trickery, like a prank conducted at school by a nemesis. She had only one thing to say at the strange face in the familiar uniform.

"No!"

"Paul?"

A voice came from behind her. Her mother brushed past and pushed open the door, and she went into the strange man's arms. Roberta watched as his hands surrounded her back and pulled her close. They said a few words—none that Roberta cared to understand. The word 'no' continued echoing in her mind, but she remained silent. Her grandmother came in behind her and placed her arm around the young girl. Her mother reopened the screen door and turned back towards them, her arm still around the man.

"Roberta, this is Paul. Paul, this is my daughter, Roberta, and my mother, Ruth."

"Pleased to see you again, Mrs. Newsom."

"It's been a long time, Paul."

"Yes, it has."

"And Roberta, you're so big. The last time I saw you was many years ago. Probably five years ago, before I moved to Chicago."

"Roberta, aren't you going to say hello?" asked her mother.

"No."

"Roberta!"

"It's all right." Paul reached inside his jacket. "Here, this is for you. Swiss chocolate. They had some at the PX before I was ready to ship out to Japan. I thought you might enjoy it."

Roberta grabbed it from his hand without saying a word and turned around and ran up the stairs like a retreating army.

"Roberta!" her mother's voice trailed after her, but she didn't care. She jumped face first onto her bed and allowed the tears from the wrong uniform to clear her mind. When she had enough crying, she turned onto her back and opened the chocolate bar. It was sweet and smooth. She hated how good it tasted. She wanted to throw it back into his face, but she thought it was too good for him. She earned it. It belonged to her, and she would devour every bite.

After a few minutes, her curiosity kicked in. She heard muffled voices from downstairs and felt a little surprised that Grandma hadn't come upstairs to inquire about her. She tiptoed down the hallway, still unable to thwart the creaks from the wooden floors, and rested on the landing, just out of view from the living room.

"I can't believe you're here."

"I wanted to surprise you."

"Well, I'm surprised."

She only heard two of them. *Were they alone?*

"I had thought you were going to the Pacific Theater."

"Those were my orders, but after the atomic bombs, everything changed ..."

Atomic bombs. She thought about the speech again and the bold headlines claiming the end of the war. *Were the bombs a good thing? They ended the war, but in doing so they brought the wrong uniform to the door.*

"I was as surprised as anyone when I received my discharge orders, and I just didn't want you to get your hopes up until I was actually on American soil."

"Paul?" Grandma's voice interrupted. "Do you like sugar in your coffee?"

"Just a little, thanks."

"I'm so happy you're here, I never expected …" Her mother stopped talking. Silence permeated the room. Roberta leaned forward to see if anyone was whispering. She heard nothing. She scooted down a step. Still nothing. Two more steps and poked her head around the side of the wall near the end of the banister. She saw her mother sitting next to Paul on the sofa. Her hand was resting on top of his. They both stared at it, perhaps unsure of what to say or do next. Roberta's stomach turned in knots, but she felt paralyzed to speak or move.

"I'm so sorry about Daniel, I …" Paul tried to say more but her mother glanced over at him and motioned for him to stop. She lifted her eyes toward Roberta, who slid out of sight behind the wall.

"Roberta. Roberta. I saw you. Come down here."

Roberta froze for a moment.

"Roberta!"

She stood and sauntered down the remaining steps, hands on the banister, and turned toward the couple on the sofa.

"The chocolate was good."

Paul chuckled. "I'm glad you liked it."

"Roberta, come sit with us," her mother said, pointing to the swivel chair across from them.

"I will. I have questions."

Grandma handed Paul his cup of coffee and settled into the unpredictable event.

Roberta kept her eyes on this man. He had brown hair, a thick jaw, and much too bushy eyebrows for her taste. They looked like caterpillars resting over his face. He smiled at her and sipped the coffee. She ignored her mother. Roberta sat on the edge of the chair and interlocked her hands in front of her.

"So, Roberta, what's your question for me?"

"First, I want to know why you wrote letters to my mother."

Mother tried to say something, but Paul interrupted with the motion of his hand as if to say the question was fine.

"Well, as you know, your father was a close friend of mine. When I heard about his death, I wanted Tricia … ahh … your mother to know I felt sorry, and I wanted her to know that if I could do anything for her—"

"Like hold her hand?"

"Roberta!"

Grandma laughed. She kind of contained it, but she couldn't hold it in completely.

"Did you see my father die?"

"No. We were in different locations."

"Are you sure that he died?"

"What do you mean?"

"How do you know if someone died if there is no body?"

Paul looked nervously over at Tricia for a moment. He started to say something then refrained. He looked lost.

"Before Daddy left, he told me he was going across the lake, and then he'd return. I'm old enough now to know that it wasn't this lake by our house."

Paul nodded but again didn't reply.

"When Grandpa Newsom died, he had a coffin. When Trigger died, he had a sack, and now he has a large rock in the backyard."

"Roberta," her mother frowned. "We have talked about this—"

"But we've never talked about it with a man in a uniform. How do you know someone has died if there is no body?"

Paul hesitated. "Reports."

"Reports?"

"There are official reports of what happened. Sometimes a body might be buried right where …" He stopped and looked at Tricia. "Should I be talking about this?"

"A body might be buried where?" asked Roberta.

Tricia nodded for Paul to continue.

"A body might be buried right where it was killed. Sometimes the body might be missing. Or it might be no more."

"How can a body be no more?"

"Fire. Explosion. Roberta, this is not good to talk about. But I'm glad you liked the chocolate. I have more at home. The next time I come—"

"No!" Roberta stood up with a defiant scowl. "No! There won't be a next time. I don't want to see that uniform ever again."

"Roberta!" scolded her mother. "You behave!"

"I don't believe that his body is no more. I don't believe he's dead. He told me he would return. Not you. You aren't supposed to be here."

"Roberta!"

"Get out! Get out!"

Grandma Newsom stepped in and put her arms around the girl. "Come, come."

"I'm going to cross the lake, and I'm going to find him. I don't want to see you again."

Her mother stood up. "I'm so sorry, Paul." He waved his hands like it was nothing. "This is appalling behavior, Roberta. Paul is my guest, and he will come whenever I want him to come. You will abide by the adult rules of this house. Do you hear me, young lady? I want you to apologize to him right now. Now, Roberta!"

Grandma Newsom prodded her from the back. Roberta glared at the wrong uniform, and spit out an airy "sorry" before her grandma led her out of the room and into the kitchen. She sat Roberta down and slid a piece of pie in front of her.

"This was going to be Paul's. But you should eat it."

Roberta picked up the crust into her hands and bit off the end. It was sweet, made from canned peaches from the previous summer.

"Don't give him any."

"You are something else, young lady."

Chapter 19

The Ring

The uniform stopped visiting Roberta's house. However, Paul did not. He wore civilian clothes. Before each visit, she would receive a sermon-length lecture on how to behave, what to say, what not to say, and the consequences she would have to endure if she didn't comply.

Roberta's stubbornness grew. There was an incident with a spoon and a pea during dinner. The pea ended up hitting Paul in the face. Roberta didn't exactly plan it that way. She only played with her food and imagined lobbing a green grenade bounding his way, but when the spoon slipped on the edge of the table and she tried to stop it from falling on the floor, the pea went flying, as if perfectly planned, and hit him in the forehead. She was grounded for a week when her explanation, true as it may have been, fell on deaf ears. She had already burned the bridge of trust.

"Get used to Paul. I like him. He's going to keep coming here," her mother said.

"Give him a chance, Roberta. He's a very nice

man," her grandma said.

"He's not ever going to replace your father," her mother said, as Paul frequented the exact chair where her father used to sit when eating dinner.

Paul kept bringing her Swiss chocolate. She accepted it each time without a word of gratitude. Her mother wouldn't allow Roberta to accept it without being polite, but Paul always insisted on her taking it anyways. She would devour it in one sitting, then continue her assault on the undercover spy who pretended to be someone different. But he couldn't fool her. She knew he had the uniform at home and all the civilian clothes in the world couldn't hide the fact. Plus, who had Swiss chocolate except someone who had been across the lake? She knew his game, and she intended to exploit him for all the chocolate he had. But it would earn him no favor.

Two weeks after the first chocolate bar appeared, he showed up at the house without the Swiss delicacy. Instead, he had in his hand a Hershey bar.

"I'm sorry, Roberta. I don't have any more Swiss chocolate."

She scoffed at the idea of replacing it with something so domestic.

"I only accept Swiss chocolate from

uniforms."

"I'm not wearing my uniform."

"But you have one. I don't want Hershey's."

She put her nose in the air and walked by him.

"I'm so sorry for her behavior," said her mother. "She's turning into a brat, and I'm ashamed of her."

She said it loud enough for Roberta to hear, but she didn't care. She kept her nose pointed upward as she climbed the stairs and sat down on the bench by the window. That's when she realized her fatal mistake. She had no chocolate. Which was more important: her pride or her desire for chocolate? She marched downstairs without saying a word, walked up to Paul, who was seated on the sofa, held out her palm and waited for the American chocolate to be placed in her hand. Without saying a word, she ascended the steps, ego bruised, but mouth about to be happy. She ignored her mother's taunts. She didn't understand.

***

A month after the new uniform showed up at the Ares' house for the first time, Roberta's mother descended the staircase wearing a sleek red dress with a broach and black shawl.

"Mom, why are you all dressed up?"

"Paul is taking me out to dinner."

"Why aren't you eating here?"

"Perhaps he's tired of flying peas and unexpected ingredients in his soup."

Two days earlier she had slid a chicken bone into his soup when he wasn't looking.

"Well, you look beautiful," Grandma said. "Roberta, doesn't she look beautiful?"

"I suppose so."

"Roberta, tell your mother how she looks for real."

"Stunning," she said with a grin and shake of the head. "I hope nobody chokes on a chicken bone."

"Roberta, your sentiments are so touching," her mother said with a sarcastic glare. "Don't wait up. Paul said we are going over to Harmorville. I might be late."

"Harmorville? That's an hour away," Grandma said.

"Which is why I said don't wait up." She walked over to Roberta and kissed her on the forehead. "What am I going to do with you?"

"What am I going to do with Paul?" replied Roberta without missing a beat.

"I suppose that is a better question. Let me know when you have an answer."

"Oh, you'll know."

"I suppose I will."

Paul arrived at the door wearing a suit and tie. He handed Roberta two chocolate bars with instructions to share with her grandma. She didn't say thank you, but took them anyway. He complimented Tricia on her dress. Roberta didn't care for how he looked at her. She grabbed the door handle and motioned with her head for them to leave, closing the door behind them.

Grandma patted Roberta on the head. "Why do you treat him so poorly? And he still gives you chocolate."

"It means he feels guilty."

"And why should he feel guilty?"

"For taking my Daddy's place."

"He's not taking your father's place?"

"Then why does he sit in daddy's chair at dinner. And he takes out Daddy's wife. And he smokes a pipe on Daddy's porch."

Grandma didn't reply, and Roberta knew why. Because Paul was taking her father's place.

***

She could hear a buzz in the kitchen the next morning. Elevated talking. Not angry. Excited. Bright. Cheery. The two women of the house bantered back and forth in a different way, and Roberta ran downstairs to see why. As she entered the kitchen, Tricia stood up from the table and smiled at Roberta. Then she held out her left hand. A ring. One single stone set into a gold band. Tricia's face beamed with satisfaction.

"Roberta, look. Paul gave me this."

A ring. What kind of ring? Why did he give it to her? She thought. She walked closer and held her mother's hand so she could inspect it.

"A diamond," her mother said.

A diamond? A diamond ring from a man. From a strange uniform.

"Roberta, Paul asked me to marry him, and I said yes."

Marry. A blank look fell across Roberta's face. She stared at the gemstone. The light shimmered from all angles. It sparkled like nothing she had ever seen except, perhaps, the sheer reflection of the lake's water on a pristine blue sky summer day.

"We are going to be wed next month."

Next month?

"I know this is a lot for you to take in, Roberta, but this will be good for our family. Paul will take care of us, all of us. He's a good man. And you're at the age when you need a strong male figure in the house. He will never replace your father, but you'll see that he will be a wonderful stepfather to you. He'll love you and take care of you and be there for you—"

Roberta refrained from yelling. She employed a tactic she'd seen many times before. She started crying, covered her face with her hands, and ran out of the room. She ran upstairs and buried her head in her pillow. It was official. Her daddy had been replaced.

This was the type of moment when grandma usually arrived and told Roberta that everything would be all right. But she didn't. It was her mother who came and sat on the edge of the bed. She didn't yell or scold or try to convince Roberta of anything. She just talked.

"Roberta, after your father died, I thought I would never love another man. I was so much in love with your father. The pain of losing him was unbearable, but as Paul and I wrote, his words and kindness were exactly what I needed. It helped me tremendously, even more so that he was friends with your father. He also loved him dearly. And I know, deep in my heart, that if your father could see us from heaven, he would want this. He would want me to be happy. He would want you to have a new father, not to replace him, but to be there when you needed someone. I know I have my faults, and I can't give you everything you need, but Paul will help. All of us. He has a good job. He will take care of us. We won't be moving anywhere. We will be here. All together, and we'll keep the memory of your father deep in our hearts every day. Every moment. That will never change. But on this earth, he is gone, and we need to move on." She paused for a moment and patted Roberta's leg. "I know this is hard. I don't expect you to accept it all today, and I want you to react however it is you are feeling. But I also want you to give Paul a chance. He's a good man, and he wants to get to know you. Please?"

She stopped talking. Roberta didn't respond. She remained face-down in her pillow until her mother left.

Roberta eventually went downstairs. She wasn't angry with her mother. She treated her pleasantly and even, on occasion, asked her mother to show her the engagement ring.

"Engagement ring. I never thought I'd ever have another one," her mother beamed. "But I never thought—"

Roberta supposed Mother was going to explain but had changed her mind.

"Mom? What's the purpose of an engagement ring?"

"It's a symbol that two people are committed

to each other, and they plan to get married."

"Is there always an engagement ring?"

"Yes. You can't get married without one. Well, that's not exactly true. But it's customary."

"Where's the ring Daddy gave you?"

"It's in my bedroom."

She wanted to ask more, but she didn't really want to know the answer. Her mother had taken off the ring given to her by her father and had replaced it with another. Roberta felt empty, and she wanted to stop the wedding, but she didn't know how.

"Roberta, we'd both like you to be in the wedding. Would you walk down the aisle right before me, holding a bouquet of flowers?"

Roberta didn't want anything to do with it.

"And we'll have a grand reception at the church hall."

She pictured Pastor Jenkins congratulating her on having a new father. It made her cringe on the inside.

"And then Paul and I will be going away for a week on our honeymoon. You'll stay with Grandma, and then when we return, Paul will move into the house with us, and we'll start a new journey as a family."

Roberta imagined watching her mother drive off and leaving her behind. Alone. Then she thought of Paul carrying his luggage up the stairs and settling into the bedroom with her mother. The horrible feeling burned a hole in her stomach. She wanted to run, but there was nowhere to go. She threw her coat on and leaned against Trigger's rock in the backyard. He would understand. He always did.

"Trigger, it's the ring. Without the ring she wouldn't be engaged and couldn't get married. But how can I get it? She wears it all the time." Trigger and her planned the next move.

"Mom?" At dinner. "Can I see the ring again?"

"Here." She put her left hand right under Roberta's face.

"It's pretty."

"I'm glad you think so. Are you warming up to the idea of Paul and marriage?"

She shrugged. "So you always wear the ring?"

"I never take it off. Well, except for my bath. I usually take my rings off for that. Nothing else. Just think, one day you'll have one of these."

She didn't relish the thought. Why would any girl want a ring that destroys her life? That puts a spell over the recipient. That was her conclusion. Mother had an evil spell cast upon her. Her mother didn't know what she was thinking and feeling, and it would be up to Roberta to stop the engagement for her own good.

Saturday morning. Her mother sat in the tub. Roberta knocked.

"Mom?"

"What is it?"

"Can I use the toilet?"

"Can't you wait?"

"What?"

"Can't you wait?"

Roberta opened the door. The curtain around the tub had been drawn. She looked like a thief on a timed-robbery, knowing that any wrong move could thwart the plan.

"What?"

"I said, 'Can't you wait?'"

She hesitated to answer. The hamper had a towel draped over the side. It sat on the towel.

"I guess so."

"Then close the door. I feel a draft." She took two steps inside and swiped it. "Roberta, what are you doing?"

"Sorry. I'm leaving now."

She closed the door behind her and ran downstairs, through the living room, out the back door in the kitchen without even saying anything to Grandma. She called after the girl, but Roberta jumped on her bicycle and coasted down the sloped driveway to the road. She rode one-handed, the other one in her pocket, clenching the prized possession. She knew where to go. She coasted into the Gulf Station.

"Jed! Jed!"

He had just finished filling up a Ford when he waved her over.

"Not a very nice day for a bike ride. Where you going?"

"There's a store in town that buys old things. I was there once. I can't remember its name or where it's at. Can you tell me?"

"You must mean McCormick's. The pawn shop."

"Yes, that's it."

"Winston Street. Two streets over from the courthouse."

"Great! Thanks."

She started pedaling when Jed called her to a stop.

"You riding there? That's more than a mile, and it kind of looks like rain."

"I don't care. I have to get there."

"What are you doing there?"

"I have something to sell."

"If you want to wait, I can drive you over in the truck in a bit."

"It can't wait. I have to go now."

"Why are you in such a hurry?"

"No reason."

"No reason?"

"Gotta go, Jed."

She had buttoned her coat pocket. She needed both hands on the handlebars for her long trip. She pedaled furiously as occasional cars honked as they passed. She had never ridden her bike to town before, nor did she think her mother would want her to do it, but it had to be done. She had thought about just throwing it away, maybe in the lake, or even on the side of the road, but she knew it had value—enough to force a new family dynamic. It must be worth something, and she wanted the money. For what? She hadn't decided yet.

Within twenty minutes, she cruised into the center of town and circled the war memorial. The town sat empty for the most part. She passed the courthouse and turned right onto Winston Street. McCormick's was three shops down. She leaned the bike against the outside wall under a large window with the words Pawn Shop written across it. She opened the door. A bell jingled. A gray-haired man with glasses and a puffy mustache looked at her from behind a counter straight ahead.

"You here alone?"

"Yes."

She approached the counter, unbuttoned her

jacket pocket, and placed the ring in front of him.

"I'd like to sell this."

He picked it up, reached for a magnifying glass and inspected the item.

"A diamond ring. Mighty pretty one. Why do you have this?"

"I want to sell it."

"Whose ring is it?"

"It's my ring."

"It looks like an engagement ring."

"Well, maybe it is. I want to sell it."

"Why do you have an engagement ring?"

"Does it matter where I got it?"

"It sure does. I once had a jealous sister storm in here and demand money for her sister's engagement ring. There ended up being a whole fight about it. I'm not here to get in the middle of anything."

"There is nothing to get in the middle of. This is my ring."

"Where did you get it?"

"My grandmother. It was her mother's. She gave it to me. I want to sell it."

"That sounds like a sentimental piece that one wouldn't sell."

"Well, I want to sell it."

"What if I don't want to buy it?"

"You don't think it's pretty?"

"I think it's very pretty. Too pretty, actually. Anyone who had it is not going to want to sell it."

"Well, I do. You want to buy it or not."

"What are you going to do with the money?"

"That's none of your business."

"Well, it is if your grandma storms in here with a shotgun demanding the ring back."

"That won't happen. My grandmother would never do that."

He looked at the ring again.

"Well, I'll give you $50 for it."

Fifty dollars! She could buy a train ticket across the country with that. She could barely contain her enthusiasm.

"All right."

"What's your name?"

"Roberta Ares."

"Ares. Your father was one who lost his life in the war, isn't that right?" She didn't answer. "I'm sorry about that. You sure this isn't your momma's ring?"

"I'm sure. This is not the ring my daddy bought for my mother. I would never sell that."

"But you would sell your grandmother's ring?"

"My fifty dollars, please."

He handed her two twenties, a five, and five ones. She handed a one back to him. "Keep this. I want some penny candy." She pointed to a display of confectioneries on her left.

"Fair trade. Diamond for candy. Fair trade indeed."

One pocket full of cash. One pocket full of candy. She felt exhilarated as she climbed back on her bike for the ride home.

"No engagement ring. No engagement. No wedding."

She repeated it over and over through the slurps of a sucker in her mouth.

"Oh no, Paul, I lost the ring. Now we can't get married."

"How could I have been so clumsy? I guess I wasn't meant to get married."

"The ring must have fallen into the tub and down the drain. Drats."

She thought of every possible reason and believed every one. But by the time she returned home and entered the house, Mother stood in the middle of the kitchen with her hands on her hips.

"Give it to me, Roberta."

"What?" She tried to remain innocent.

"I know you took it. Off the hamper when you came into the bathroom this morning. Give it to me now."

"What, mom?"

"The engagement ring. What did you do with

it?"

"Mom, did you lose it down the drain?"

"Roberta! Where have you been for the past hour?"

"I rode to town to get candy."

"You aren't supposed to ride to town. And where did you get the money for candy?"

"Grandma gave it to me."

"No, I didn't," Grandma said, entering the kitchen from the living room.

"Roberta, you're already in hot water. Just give me back the ring before you get into more trouble."

"I don't have the ring."

"You rotten little girl."

Her mother reached for her jacket and felt her pockets. She tugged on the edge of the jacket as she unbuttoned the left pocket, flinging fistfuls of candy onto the floor.

"Roberta!"

Then she pulled the other side of the jacket towards her. Roberta flinched backwards, but her mother grabbed her arm and flipped open the flap of the second pocket. Then she reached in and pulled out the handful of bills.

"Roberta, what did you do?"

The girl lashed out with every emotion in her chest. "I got rid of the ring so you wouldn't be engaged anymore, so you couldn't get married. It's gone."

Tricia grabbed Roberta by the collar and smacked her behind with her right hand.

"You evil child." She hit her again. "What did you do with it? Tell me."

She spanked her again.

Roberta cried and fell onto the floor.

"What did you say?"

"McCormick's."

Tricia walked out of the house without her coat, money clenched in her left hand. Roberta heard the car start and pull out of the driveway. She laid flat on the kitchen floor in a full-on cry, her grandma standing over her.

Chapter 20

The Church

After the ring incident, a full week had passed before the spoken forgiveness and the behavior of the members of the house finally coincided with each other. For the first few days after purchasing back the ring for twice the amount—McCormick's assured her she was still getting quite a deal—Roberta's mother gave daily, and sometimes, hourly lectures to the girl, who mostly took it with a dour face. She never responded. She descended inside her mind and lived at a distance from those around her. School, home, chores. Nothing more. She would sit in the back yard and talk to Trigger's rock. It always understood what she was feeling even if she didn't.

Roberta did apologize. And yes, she did acknowledge she had done something wrong. She stole the ring. She knew what Pastor Jenkins had taught about stealing. She had lied about it, which was something related to bears and false witnessing, again from Pastor Jenkins. She had ridden her bike to town without permission.

Pastor Jenkins never spoke about that one, but apparently it was wrong too. Beyond all of her other sins, she had hatred for the man replacing her father. This was the only way she was able to explain it. The transformation continued day after day, and she felt helpless to stop it.

On the day before the wedding, she had been bullied into submission by squawking voices of excitement. Tricia's two best friends spent the entire day at the house, gawking over the details, the dress, the wedding cake, the bouquets. Roberta endured every bubbly comment.

"Isn't it exciting, Roberta? That your mother's getting married?"

"It's so wonderful, Roberta, that you'll have a step-father like Paul. He's a wonderful man."

"Oh, Roberta, you'll look so beautiful in this dress, carrying the flowers down the church's center aisle."

She shrugged them all off with fake smiles and half-lies about being busy getting ready for the day. She even felt the distance from Grandma, who clearly had shifted into the pro-wedding camp.

"Roberta, I know you've had your difficulties, but please, for your mother's sake, and for mine, do you promise not to make a scene at the wedding? Do you promise to show her the respect that she deserves?"

She nodded. "I promise."

"And do you promise to give Paul a chance."

She couldn't.

"Or at least don't be difficult for him. Give him some time. You'll warm up to him."

Don't be difficult. Roberta knew what that really meant. Don't express her true feelings. Hide them deep down. Don't act out. Don't steal rings. Don't cry out. Don't …

Grandma cooked an extravagant meal for the entire wedding group on the evening before. They sat around the dining room table full of laughter and opened wine bottles, and ate Grandma's famous homemade pasta. Roberta sat by herself in a dress, on the swivel chair. She didn't want to eat. She wanted to hear their talk and understand what part of her life she was losing.

Her mother tucked her in that night and kissed her on the forehead. She seemed especially happy, and Roberta didn't want to say anything to change that.

"I love you, Mom."

She meant it. She's not exactly sure why she said it. It had been a while since such sentiments had rolled off her tongue, and at least the same while since her mother had reciprocated in kind.

But the tenderness softened her mother's already emotionally happy face a little more. Her mother gushed about her love for her daughter, and she talked about the long difficult year, but how happiness in the family was possible. Paul. Paul. Paul. She said several things about Paul. Always connected with happiness. As she left the room, Roberta felt alone. Not physically alone like she was each night. Mentally alone, in her thoughts, her orphaned thoughts which deviated from the prevailing wind of the house. Her thoughts of Paul had no connection to happiness—only to a uniform promising it would come home but never did.

She fell asleep and dreamed. She sat in the pew of the church. All alone. Pastor Jenkins entered from the vestibule and stood in front of the pulpit. He motioned for someone to move towards him. At that moment, Roberta was no longer on the pew but stood in the back of the center aisle, flowers in hand, and Pastor Jenkins waved for her to come. Music started playing. Her feet wanted to walk forward according the cadence of the beat, but her mind refused her legs, and she stood deviant, unwilling to bridge the distance between them. She felt a nudge from behind. It was her mother in a wedding dress, veil over her face. She could barely see her expression.

She told her to go. To walk forward, but the white wedding dress lifted into the air, her mother was gone, and the dress morphed into the white-winged creature, the same one she saw in the water. The creature floated backwards toward the double-doors to the outside world. It wanted her to move, but the opposite way. Run away with her. Go outside. Roberta dropped the flowers in the middle of the aisle and ran towards the door, her mind blank except for one thing—the freedom of the outdoors. As she pushed the doors open, her head emerged above the surface of the water. Her hair dripping wet. She looked up at the blue sky and treaded alone on the surface. She felt peace and the white-winged creature lifted slowly into the atmosphere until it disappeared out of sight, like an airplane which had peaked over the horizon. Beside her, the airplane, the one sent to her by her father, floated in a steady pattern on the dips and dives of the water's surface. She reached for it and jolted awake. The morning light had begun to brighten her room. It was the morning of the wedding.

Two of her mother's friends had spent the night. They bustled and hustled throughout the morning, fretting over details and any imperfection which still had time to be righted. Roberta stayed out of the way. She did what she was told, helped as minimally as possible, lied about how excited she was, and dreaded the moment when she would have to walk directly down the aisle towards a smiling Paul, waiting for his bride.

They piled into two cars at ten o'clock and drove to the church. Roberta wore a dark blue dress that Grandma had made specifically for the wedding. For that purpose, and that purpose alone, she hated it.

The organ played as the attendees waited patiently. Roberta stood in the foyer, clutching an item in her hand. She had carried it from home, not showing it to anyone, and as the foyer doors opened to the sanctuary, and as her first glimpse of Paul settled onto her chest, she opened her fist. The wings from the uniform, given to her on Christmas Eve by the man who brought the terrible news, glared back at her, and she pinned it on the left side of her dress under her shoulder. She had wings now, and would allow them to take her where they willed.

She swallowed hard and felt a nudge from behind. Sweaty, heavy breathing, eyes upon her. Another nudge. The voice from her mother. She couldn't. She turned and ran towards the double doors; she could sense herself emerging over the surface of the water. She didn't want to drown.

She wanted to be free, to fly through the air, to cross the lake, to search for the downed plane on the other side.

As she opened the door into the cool November air, her grandmother stopped her. She wasn't sure if she had been waiting as a sentry outside the church or if she had witnessed the weak-kneed girl and had predicted the run, but she was there to stop the child. That's what she still was. She had grown up too much in one year, but she was at heart still Daddy's little girl.

"Roberta."

Tears formed in the wild child's eyes. "I can't, Grandma."

"Yes, you can. Do you love your mother?"

"Yes."

"Then do this for her. I know it isn't fair. You're too young to lose a father and to have to worry about a changing family. It's not fair to you, but this is life, Roberta. I think you want your mother to be happy, don't you?"

"Yes."

"And you trust your mother to do what's right for your family?"

"Yes."

"And you know that she loves you?"

"Yes."

"Do this for her. Make her happy, even if you

aren't."

Her grandma wiped the tears under the child's eyes. The same eyes which agreed with the assessment. She turned to see her mother in white, waiting for her, arms reaching out, music still playing in the background, hundreds of expectant eyes waiting to find out what would happen.

Roberta reached out and took her mother's hand. The Maid of Honor had picked up the bouquet and handed it back to her. She gripped the bottom of the bouquet tightly, then took the first step into the sanctuary, towards a future she couldn't prevent. Within a minute, she stood off to the left of Paul, and her mother had filled the space between them, but she looked at him, not her. The pastor spoke the words, most of which Roberta did not hear. She was lost in her thoughts, lost in the space above the church, the wide-open spaces, and the flowing breeze which blew her hopes to some distant shore she would never reach.

"And by the power invested in me, I now pronounce you husband and wife. You may kiss the bride."

They kissed to make it official. She had a step-father, and a mother with a divided heart.

Some people lose their appetite when their

mind is occupied. Roberta was opposite. She had four pieces of wedding cake at the reception in the church hall. Her mother kissed her goodbye and said that they would stop by the house in the morning to say goodbye again before they took their train trip for their honeymoon.

"We're staying at a hotel in town tonight. But we'll see you in the morning."

Later in the night, Grandma tucked her in and asked her how she felt. She smiled and said everything was fine. She would see them in the morning. Grandma kissed her on the cheek and left the room. She still held the wings in her hand and wondered what it would be like to truly fly freely without anything holding her down. She wanted to be a pilot, like her father, and she would fly far away from home and perhaps, too, never come back.

Chapter 21

The Trek

The morning after the wedding, she woke early to a quiet house. Mother, the new wife, hadn't returned yet. Morning broke gently over the lake. The wet air hung over Trigger's rock like a fog of war claiming another victim.

She hadn't dreamed during the night, not like the previous evening. She lie trapped in her bed, unable to express any of her emotions, other than the words her tears spoke for her. She thought of the lake, of her father, and of the butterfly which had long been out of her memory. She thought of the ice and slipping through it, the boat and falling from it. She thought of her mother laughing with Paul, holding hands with Paul, kissing Paul. She only had one journey left to take, and she thought with all her heart that no one would care if she took it. Perhaps they'd even be happier.

She pushed away the blankets and sat in the chair by the desk. She wrote a note: *Mom, it's all right. You can have Paul. I know that's who you want.*

I will have Daddy. Love, Roberta.

She knew to dress warm in November with the evenings dipping into the 30s. She put on her long underwear, the same ones she wore skating in the winter. She put on a work dress, a shirt and sweater. She filled a small linen bag with a few more items of clothing and sneaked out of the bedroom grasping the bag and her airplane. She paused in the middle of the hallway. She heard Grandma snoring. The other bedroom was empty. But not for long. Soon there would be a husband and wife there, and she couldn't bear to think about it. She returned to her bedroom and reached under the bed for Trigger's leash. It hadn't been used in nearly a year. She would bring it with her because she knew that Trigger would have loved to come. He would have eagerly followed her anywhere, so she played tribute to her best friend while thinking that a rope might prove useful on a journey. She walked back down the hallway and descended the staircase. She packed several muffins Grandma had made the morning before, put on her coat, and placed the note on the kitchen table. She slowly opened the door in small increments to minimize the creaking. She made it outside.

She walked through the wet grass to Trigger's rock and stood solemnly beside it.

"You were the best, Trigger. I know you will wish me luck. I wish you could come with me."

She kissed the plaque, circled the house, crossed the street, and walked directly to the edge of the lake. Light from the sky had just begun to hit the lake's eastern shore, painting the tops of the distant trees in an iridescent white glow.

She would go there and see. It was the only decision which made any sense.

The war wasn't over there, she said to herself. But it didn't matter. This was *the* lake. The lake her father brought her to. He crossed it nonetheless, and even if she couldn't find him, she would be closer, she thought. That's all she wanted. But she also knew in her heart that she would find him. She had to. He's all she had left.

She didn't know how to find the other side of the lake, but she knew not to walk towards town. The lake wrapped itself around the belly of the town, and if she walked that way, she could be found easily by anyone on the main road. So she would go to the left, into the woods, through the barren trees. She would follow the edge of the lake, keeping it in view at all times, and if she did so, she reasoned, she would eventually be there, amongst the trees on the other side.

She trudged out of the manicured park lawn and into the matted leaves of the wet woods. She crossed through a yard or two of some houses which buttressed up against the lake. One had a big dog that chased her from behind for a hundred yards or so. But she escaped through the brush while keeping an eye on the lake at all times.

She missed Grandma and her old mother. The pre-Paul mother. But that wasn't actually true. She thought more. Pre-Christmas mother. She hadn't been the same since the two uniforms arrived on Christmas Eve. She missed the mother who didn't cry, who didn't run out of the room, who didn't need a letter from a different man in a different uniform. That's the mother she missed, the one who rested on her thoughts. But useless thoughts would get her nowhere. That mother had changed, and so had Roberta. She had a place to discover. She had to be brave.

"I can't fall through the ice this time."

There was no ice.

"I can't fall out of a boat."

She only had her boots and one step after the other.

She rested after a while on a log and ate a muffin. She missed Trigger's companionship and could have used it at the moment.

"Don't worry, Trigger. I'll come back one day. I won't forget you. I won't forget to visit your rock. I'll be back. After my journey is complete."

She heard herself ask, *When. When will she return*? She didn't have an answer.

"Stop. No more thinking. I have to go. Follow the lake."

She trekked over felled logs and through marshy land that started to seep into her boots. She knew it wasn't good to have wet feet. Grandma would always have her take off her clothes and warm her feet by the fire after a round of ice skating. She wondered how she would be able to dry them. She couldn't think about it now. She had to keep moving.

After another fifteen minutes of slow progress as the gray sky gave up as much light as it couldn't prevent, she stopped in realization and said out loud: "Where's my airplane?" She had forgotten it. She had allowed a muffin to steal her attention, and as she continued moving forward, she had left the airplane sitting alone on the forest floor. She thought about going back but couldn't bear the thought of retracing her steps.

"Airplane down. Airplane down! But I'm alright. I parachuted out before its crash. Repeat, there are survivors."

She thought about that. She had survived an airplane crash, why couldn't Daddy? She knew it was silly to think this way, but she couldn't help it. The thoughts overwhelmed her.

"Step after step." She moved forward.

More than an hour into her journey, the slope of the land had risen to a point where she looked down upon the lake from a tall hill. As she peered ahead, the trees seemed to be separated, like a final row was planted before an open-air expanse. As she approached the row of trees which had no ground beyond them, she realized she stood on a natural culvert, a mini-canyon with a white-water stream at the bottom which cascaded into the lake. She looked as far as she could to her left but there was no easy way across—no bridge, no natural walkway, only jagged rocks and tufts of grass placed precariously on the side of the bank.

Now what? She thought of her options—going back not being one of them. She could follow the bank to her left and see if it would provide for a way across, or she could climb down the side of the bank and jump over the water using the rugged rocks which nearly dammed the stream.

"Roberta, you've come this far. The other side of the lake might be right on the other side of this stream. Cross. Just cross. Don't be afraid."

She turned her right foot to the side and allowed it to slide down the crest of the bank a few inches until it rested on a rock poking out of the dirt.

"Step after step."

She centered her entire weight on the rock then lifted her right foot again to position it against a clod of grass below it. She maneuvered herself inch by inch down the incline. If it wasn't for the large rocks calling to her from the bottom, she might have just sat down and allowed gravity to take her, but she thought it prudent to be slower and more methodical.

On her fourth attempt to move lower, the rock she had chosen as the anchor for her right foot dislodged itself, sending her entire body on an unencumbered slip downward. Her head flailed outward, as did her arms, and she screamed as she fell hard amongst a series of rocks on the bank of the stream.

She noticed sound first. The trickling of the water loud in her ears as if she had poked her head into the middle of a waterfall. She opened her eyes, and the gray sky hung over her like a dirty linen sheet from a front-line triage center. Then she felt the pain in her left leg; it throbbed, and each time she tried to move it, she scrunched her nose and thought of the time she fell from the tree in her backyard and broke her leg. Daddy was there that day, and he carried her to the car and drove her to the doctor's office.

Her head throbbed. She reached with her left hand to the back of her skull and felt wetness in her hair. She held her hand in front of her eyes. Red. Blood. She closed her eyes just to make sure she wasn't dreaming. But the sound of the water and the pain of her body assured her that she had fallen onto the side of the stream. If she had fallen in it, she would have drowned.

She had no idea how long she had been lying there. It could have been three minutes or three hours for that matter. Either way, she had trouble getting the energy to lift her head and sit-up so she could look at her foot. She counted to three, placed her palm onto the cold, wet ground and pushed off to try to get into the seated position, but no luck. She lay at the mercy of the elements, near the side of the lake which had now almost killed her three times in less than a year. It was at that moment that she realized she was part of the war herself. No doubt. Everyone was.

It took her five minutes to gain the momentum to talk.

"Hello," her voice rumbled low. "Hello."

Who would be helping her on a day like this?

"Help." It grew louder as her lungs began to expand. "Help." She grew more confident, perhaps from the fear now gripping her chest. "Help!" What was her other option? She couldn't move. She couldn't sit up. She was far off the beaten path. Her voice remained her only option, and she would use it.

"Help!"

Again and again.

"Help!"

She called repeatedly, minute after minute, the unspecified clicks of the clock continued unabated as her impassioned cry matched it in cadence and consistency.

"Help!"

Ten minutes was an hour. An hour a lifetime. She thought of her daddy alone, across the lake, perhaps trapped in a field, yelling for help, and she cried, bawling through the yells of rescue, wanting nothing more than to be in her own bed than to sit at her desk and look out upon the rock, to have her mother hold her in her arms and her grandmother to greet her in the morning with a loving kiss and a hot stack of pancakes. She was sorry for everything but mostly sorry for her daddy all alone.

"Roberta!"

She lifted her eyes upward. *A man. Father? Did he come? An angel?* He held an airplane in his hands. Her airplane.

"Roberta!"

"Daddy!"

"I'm coming."

The man slid off the top of the bank, using all four limbs to balance and climb down.

She kept yelling for him. He kept assuring her that he was coming. He reached the bottom and stood over her.

"Where's my airplane?"

"I left it on the top of the bank."

"Daddy?"

"I got you, Roberta."

But his face didn't match the frame on the mantle. She looked again.

"Paul?"

"Shhhh. Don't worry. I'm gonna get you out of here."

The newlywed pulled a handkerchief out of his pocket and wrapped it around her head.

"You hit your head, but you aren't bleeding anymore. Don't move."

"My foot."

He looked down at her left leg. "You probably have a broken ankle. You won't be able to walk."

"How will I get out of here?"

"You let me worry about that. That's what soldiers do. We always say never leave a soldier behind, but sometimes we have to. Like your father, and it hurts us more than anything. But if there's a way, we'll move heaven and earth to make sure he's brought back to safety. And that's what we're going to do right now. I'm gonna sit down beside you, and I want you to lift your arms onto my back as high as you can, all right?"

"Yes."

She did. She felt his hands reach around. "A little higher. Can you reach my neck?"

"Yes."

He put both hands behind him, onto the sides of her torso, and lifted at once with his arms and his body, shifting back and forth until he grunted and stood up with Roberta hanging off his back. He put his hands under her for support.

"You all right?"

"Yes."

"Let's get out of here."

He climbed the bank an inch at a time, a stable rock, a clump of grass, a slide down two inches and a jump up three until he reached the top, and they rested, Roberta sitting in his lap with his legs hanging off the top of the bank.

"Where's Mommy?" Roberta had tears streaming down her face, but she cried quietly.

"She went with your grandma in the car looking for you. But I had a hunch where you might be, and then I found your airplane right along the edge of the lake."

"I'm sorry."

"Shhhh. Let's get you home. Your mother is so worried about you."

"I'm sorry I ruined your honeymoon."

"Shhhh. Roberta. We're family. We always have been. Your father was like a brother to me. I would have done anything for him, and now the best I can do is to make sure his little girl is happy and safe. That's all he ever wanted. He loved you so much."

She placed her head on his shoulder and closed her eyes.

"All right," he said. "This isn't going to be easy. We have a long way back, so let's get started. Here. You wanna carry the airplane?"

"Yes."

She grasped it in her hands and they walked through the trees, Roberta gingerly held over Paul's shoulder.

***

He emerged from the woods into the lawn of a neighbor, one hundred yards from home. He staggered past the quiet house with two prying eyes and up the bank onto the pavement. He hadn't stopped once, Roberta had noticed, but she heard his heavy breathing and the shakiness of his arms. As he approached home, his steps quickened, past the spot where dead Trigger once lay, along the sidewalk and up the steps of the porch. Through the glass window, she caught a glimpse of her mother, who ran towards her, tore open the door and screamed a cry of relief with tears. Grandma followed her, and the exhausted ex-soldier placed her on the sofa, and plopped down on the floor next to her. Mother and Grandma attended every wound and bruise, seemingly their intuition told them what hurt. Roberta didn't speak. There lacked a need for it. She smiled despite the pain and knew she had made it back. She hadn't been to the other side, not really, but she felt she understood it a little better. Paul turned and his smile caught hers, which didn't turn, but remained a painted moment in time for all the moments yet to come, thanks to him.

Chapter 22

Christmas Eve '45

In the three and a half weeks leading up to Christmas Eve '45 following Roberta's traumatic trek, she wrestled the varied answers she had to the questions in her mind.

Who was this Paul? Conclusion: A man who loved her mother very much.

Why was Mother happy? Because Paul loved her.

Why wasn't Mother angry at her for running away? Love. Her safety meant more to her mother than anything else. Roberta even supposed her mother loved her even more than Paul.

If these were the only questions her mind had in the aftermath, serenity would have returned, and she would have mellowed herself into the precious obedient girl she had always been.

But Roberta had noticed a new dynamic in her life: bold moves receive bold attention. She grasped the power and refused to abdicate.

Honeymoon? Canceled.

They attended her wounds without yelling or maternal lectures. Just kindness. Only love.

Blankets and soup for the warmth. Paul deservingly received the royal treatment, too. What Roberta found to be curious was how it was Paul who emphatically canceled the honeymoon.

"We're not going anywhere. I'll call in the morning to refund our train tickets. We're a family now, so let's start living like one right away."

The declaration of common family startled the young ailing girl, but secretly it comforted her. A man had endured the harsh weather and canceled his honeymoon for a girl who didn't even like him—who hadn't even given him one ounce of respect or kindness—who turned her nose up at him and ignored him. Why? Why would he do that? Answer: he loved her mother. What did that fact mean to Roberta? She wasn't sure.

Mutual love meant Paul would stay. Forever.

She hadn't broken any bones, only badly sprained her ankle. The first two nights after the incident she slept downstairs on the sofa because she refused to allow Paul to carry her to her room. What was the big deal? He had carried her all the way back from the bottom of the canyon, and she was grateful for it, but she didn't want him to touch her. However, that also meant that she had to relieve herself into a metal basin. After two days of self-humiliation and painful squatting in the living room, she requested Grandma to ask Paul to carry her upstairs at night. Grandma said, "Ask him yourself." Roberta glared. "Paul …"

He came to her like her servant and carried her upstairs at night, downstairs in the morning, and up again twice during the day to take care of her daily duties. She still had trouble smiling at him and thanking him, though she felt gratitude in her heart for having a toilet to use.

As Christmas approached and Roberta's leg began to heal, a cloud of uncertainty hung over the household: how would they react to the first anniversary of the death? Grandma prepared Roberta to be sensitive to her mother on this "first Christmas since she heard about your father's passing."

Her mother seemed more focused on getting Roberta to like Paul. "Play a game with him. Talk to him."

Roberta shrugged her off as she did with his approaches, too.

"Roberta, would you like to …"

"No thank you."

"Roberta, I fixed the wing on your airplane."

"Thank you."

"We could go outside and play with it if you like."

"No thank you."

"Roberta, I've been wondering what you would like for a Christmas gift."

"No thank you."

"Roberta ..."

"No."

It made her feel guilty. Each time she said no to him, she would remember how he held her in his arms and carried her out of the forest. He saved her life. She knew it but couldn't reconcile that with his occupying the place where her father should have been.

On Sunday December 23, the entire family attended the evening church service. Roberta walked down the aisle unencumbered except for a slight limp. It was the first time she had returned to church since the wedding, and she felt the eyes still upon her. Pastor Jenkins reminded the flock that a year had ended since the death of one of their own. He recounted the horrible phone call he received last Christmas Eve. With Tricia's permission he stated how the year had shown God's faithfulness, the miraculous rescue of Roberta from the lake, and the wedding that had seemingly blessed every soul of the town except Roberta. She felt exposed by the language, and wondered why Mother had allowed such openness, though she was glad he hadn't mentioned the aftermath of the wedding and her treacherous trek.

"Mrs. Ares has asked to say a few words."

Roberta jolted her head towards Mother, who stepped into the aisle and walked to the front of the church. The first thought that struck Roberta was that her mother still had the name Mrs. Ares, even though her new husband had a different name. She couldn't understand the significance. She also feared what her mother would say in front of the congregation. At that moment, they all felt like strangers, and she glanced around at the curious eyes. Robbie Dwyer sat across the aisle from her. He gawked at her like an animal at the carnival. Like he couldn't imagine a child without a father, who received a new father and now had a mother who was going to talk openly about their lives in front of the entire town. Roberta assured herself those were indeed Robbie's thoughts.

"Thank you, Pastor Jenkins. I just wanted to publicly state to all of you, that this community has been my family this past year. Your support, prayers, kind words, gifts, and friendship have meant the world to me. As you know, tomorrow is the one-year anniversary of losing my beloved Daniel, the father of my child. This is not the path I wanted to walk. I'll admit I've been far too weak this year, sometimes unsure if I could even go on.

But the things that sustained me were my faith, my friends, and my family."

She paused and looked directly at Roberta. The smile sat comfortably on her face. Mother didn't cry. She seemed confident. Happy.

"And through this grief, God has unexpectedly blessed me with another good man, Paul, who can be the father figure that my daughter needs …"

Father figure. She didn't understand what exactly that meant. Father figure. It had the word father in it. But she still called him Paul, and as far as she knew, that's all he would ever deserve. He couldn't be a father. What was a figure of a father?

She missed the entire end of her mother's speech as she wrestled with semantics. As her mother sat down, she leaned over and asked: "What's a father figure?"

Mother answered without pause. "Someone who is not your father, but loves you like a father."

She looked at Paul, who listened to Pastor Jenkins. *Does he love me like a father? How could he ever love me like my real daddy?*

***

On Christmas Eve morning, Roberta woke

with a resolution to share. "I don't want any Christmas presents."

"Why?"

"I want daddy's airplane to be the last gift I ever received." She looked at Paul in that moment as a way of emphasis. Grateful or not for what he did, she decided she didn't want a new father or a father figure. She would do fine without him, so he could go on living in the house and sitting at Daddy's place at the table but nothing more.

Of course, she displayed flawed logic. She had received gifts on her birthday, but she didn't care about glaring inconsistencies. On this day, the bi-winged airplane was all that mattered.

"Roberta," said Grandma. "Santa Claus might have already gotten you a surprise. Don't you think you'd at least like to see what it is tomorrow morning before you reject it?"

"No, Grandma. I can reject it now. The airplane was the perfect gift. I need nothing more." She looked back at Paul.

"Roberta, you're being ridiculous and a little rude," stated her mother. "Why do you have to be like this?"

Her mother excused herself from the room. It was the first time she had done so in many months. Paul went after her, but soon returned, tongue-tied to such a degree that he ate two of

Grandma's muffins in silence. Eventually, he let out a long sigh.

"Roberta, you're right to think so highly of your father. If you want the airplane to be the last gift you ever receive, I think that is quite meaningful."

She hated when he agreed with her.

"Grandma, I'm going outside to play. By myself."

Bundled in her wool coat, she leaned against Trigger's rock as flurries swirled around her. She read the plaque, and felt a tinge of pain in her stomach. Not physical pain. Nervousness, and she asked Trigger how it felt to be dead. She still wanted to know. Not for herself but for her father.

She wandered around the side of the house, across the street, and stood at the edge of the lake, which had yet to freeze over. This was the first time she had come to the lake since she ran away. She glimpsed the far-off shore and wondered how close she had gotten to her destination. She remembered a large local map at the Gulf Station, and she would ask Jed the next time she saw him to help her identify the canyon. She turned towards the house once and noticed her mother standing on the porch with only a sweater on, arms crossed. Roberta looked at her, and they each waved to one another. A gentle wave. A wave that didn't need to be defined, not on that day. Roberta glanced back at the lake, but when she turned again, her mother had gone into the house almost as if to say that she trusted her. She knew she wasn't going to attempt a crossing.

The quiet day dragged to evening. A fire roared. They made small talk with cookies and popcorn as they waited for the Christmas Eve radio drama.

Mother had turned on the radio but quickly turned it off again. She had her head down for a moment then faced the other three. Roberta could tell she had something important to say.

"I would like to light a candle to remember Daniel—Daddy. And I'd like to place it on the mantle to watch it burn this evening while we're here together. Would anyone else like to do this with me?"

"Yes, I would," said Grandma.

Paul concurred.

Now it was up to Roberta. "Yes."

Paul lit the first one, and each of them held the finger ring of the candelabra in a slight horizontal bent and lit theirs with Paul's flame. They placed them all on the mantle, Roberta, wanting to do it herself, needed a chair to safely reach it, and then sat quietly watching the flickering as the radio drama punched out the typical Christmas tropes that made them chuckle far less than usual.

When the radio show finished, Grandma read *Twas a Night Before Christmas* and a passage from the Bible. Then Paul spoke.

"You know, Christmas was the loneliest time for a soldier at war. Miserable. But to have thoughts of a loving family waiting for you. To have a dream that one day you could be sitting by a fire and a Christmas tree, to be near the people you love, that's all a soldier wants. I feel I don't deserve this—this beautiful but difficult evening. I wish Daniel could be here. I truly do. I don't deserve this, but thank you for making me part of your family. I can't tell you how much it means to me."

Mother reached over and took his hand. Roberta kept her eyes on the candles, munching slowly on the popcorn in front of her. Paul surprised her with his revelation that he was out of place and undeserving of the seat on the sofa. He knew. Roberta couldn't imagine what that meant.

As the evening dwindled, Grandma said goodnight leaving the three to watch the candles get smaller.

"Mom?"

"Yes."

"Can I stay up until all the candles go out?"

"Yes."

"Can it just be me and you?"

Paul nodded and leaned over and kissed Tricia on the cheek. "I'm going to go to bed." He reached down and patted Roberta's head. "Goodnight, Roberta."

"Goodnight."

Roberta slid up next to Mother.

"Roberta, is there anything you want to talk about? Anything about Daddy?"

"I miss him."

"So do I."

Mother started crying and the tears elicited more from Roberta. She hadn't cried for her daddy in a longtime, but the memories flooded her mind. The knock at the door. The uniforms. Her mother collapsing onto the floor. The dog. The rock. The entire year which held them captive.

They held each other late into the evening. Sometimes with tears. Sometimes with small talk and even a spattering of laughter. As the candles flickered out one by one, they fell asleep next to each other on the floor by the fireplace. The embers kept them warm until the grim dark night felt the coldness once more.

Chapter 23

Christmas in '45

She awakened on the floor with a pillow under her head and a blanket tucked around her. The smell of fresh-baked-something lifted her expression and nose, a sure sign Grandma worked in the kitchen. Embers still crackled in the fireplace. She glanced up and noticed the four melted candles sitting idly on the mantle. The tree to her right had presents under it, and she crawled out from under the covers until she could reach the first one in front of her. The tag read Roberta.

"I guess Santa Claus didn't listen to your request." Her mother stood behind her with a mug of hot cocoa in her hand. "Merry Christmas."

"Merry Christmas, Mom."

"Hope it's alright if you got a couple presents? Guess Santa Claus is as stubborn as a ten-year-old girl I know."

Roberta smiled. "Is there more hot cocoa?"

"What do you think? Grandma's in the kitchen."

Before she could move, Paul plodded down the stairs and stopped at the landing at the bottom.

"I need everyone to get their coats and come with me."

Grandma popped her head in the living room from the kitchen. "I have cinnamon rolls hot out of the oven."

"Pack them and bring them."

"We have to open presents," Roberta said.

"I thought you didn't want any presents." She hated that Paul responded exactly how she would have. "This is very important. Everyone needs to come with me."

"But Paul," said Mother. "We have traditions we usually follow on Christmas morning and ..."

"I realize this is unorthodox ..."

"What's that mean?" asked Roberta.

"Out of the ordinary. But this is very important. For all of us."

"I don't want to go," Roberta stated, almost with a flare of defiance.

"But," continued Paul, "... this is especially important for you, Roberta."

"What is it?"

"I can't tell you. I have to show you."

"But I don't want to."

"Roberta," her mother pointed at her. "Let's

go with Paul and find out."

"Do you know what it is, Mom?"

"I don't."

Paul put on his coat. "Roberta, do this for me, please? Just this one thing."

"Why should I do this for you?" Roberta snapped. She knew she sounded like a spoiled brat, but she didn't care.

"Roberta," her grandmother spoke up. "This man saved your life, for crying out loud! He's asking you to go with him on Christmas morning. It must be important. Now get your coat."

"Grandma—"

"Now!"

Grandma didn't speak to her in such a forceful manner very often. She obeyed. *What could he possibly want? Why would it interest me?* Those were her two questions as she put her coat on and her mother wrapped a scarf around her.

"Thank you all. Thank you," Paul said. "Our first Christmas together, I want it to be our most memorable. Just wait. Come, come. Oh, and Roberta, those wings you have that you sometimes pin on your coat, bring them."

"Why?"

"You need them."

Enthusiasm reverberated in his voice—an optimism not typically displayed as Roberta trudged upstairs for the wings and as he herded everyone into the car. Grandma sat in the backseat with Roberta. They pulled out of the driveway and turned right toward town. They passed the shuttered Gulf Station, which made Roberta wonder about the map of the lake on the wall inside.

"Where are we going? Everything is closed on Christmas."

"Not everything."

They entered town. An overnight snow had painted its fringes a bright white, like a painting had come to life. Roberta couldn't deny its beauty. Grandma effused with praise for the scene as she opened the basket of rolls and passed them around. Roberta bit into the fresh cinnamon bun as the car circled the war memorial in front of the courthouse and scooted behind it, passing Winston Street, where she had once sold an engagement ring for a pocket full of penny candy. She glanced down the barren street but said nothing.

The car traveled several more blocks until the lake came into view. Paul turned on Lake Drive and followed the shore out of town for several miles until he turned onto another road, which Roberta didn't ever remember traveling on.

"Where are we going?"

"Roberta, let's just enjoy the ride," said Grandma.

"Do you know where, Grandma?"

"No."

Mother concurred with Grandma's assessment. "Yes, beautiful snow, cinnamon rolls, family time; what more could you want?"

Roberta knew the answer to that question but didn't dare say.

The road wound around the lake and sauntered through sloping hills with pockets of trees creating intermittent glimpses of the water. The car ride approached forty minutes as Paul pulled across the road and parked on a patch of dirt amidst a cluster of trees on both sides of the road. Roberta noticed a stake in the ground with a red cloth tied to it.

"What's the red cloth for?"

"Ah," Paul answered. "I put it there so I'd know where to stop."

"What is this place?" asked Mother.

"We need to do a little exploring. Roberta, how's your foot feeling today? I can carry you into the woods if that will help."

"No thank you. But why are we going into the woods?"

"I have something to show you. All of you."

The vacant road lay as the well-trodden path

in both directions, but they would veer off and encounter the uncharted. They stepped onto a bank into the the woods.

"I probably should have told you to wear your boots," Paul said.

"I didn't know we were going hiking," Mother sneered. "I'm not prepared for this."

"It's not long. Trust me."

He gave a hand to Grandma and helped her up a small incline. He asked if Roberta needed a hand, but she managed herself. When they reached the top, they looked down through the barren brown trees touching into the gray sky with their bare branches. Through the maze they could see it.

"The lake."

"Yes. Come. Down here just a little ways. To the clearing near the shore."

Paul goaded them around a few fallen trees and into the wide-open area near the edge of the lake.

"What are we doing here?" asked Roberta.

"Yes, we could have just looked at the lake from our house and been much warmer," said Mother with a faint hint of a complaint.

"Yes, we could have, but we wouldn't be able to see it from this vantage point." He reached into his pocket, pulled out a tightly wrapped package, and handed it to Roberta. It felt heavy. "Sorry, I didn't listen to you. I bought you something."

"What is it?"

"Open it."

Roberta removed her mittens and handed them to Grandma. She tore open the end of the package and flipped the cardboard flap so she could slide out a pair of black binoculars.

"Binoculars?"

"To help you see, Roberta. Look there." He pointed.

She put them over her eyes.

"Adjust it here."

He showed her how to move the eye piece for a clear view. As she turned the right lens, she caught a glimpse of it. Clearly. Her house. She moved the left lens to create the perfectly adjusted image. She could see the porch, and she panned down to look at the park where she stood just yesterday. Then it hit her. She had arrived. On the other side. She had crossed the lake, and she knew in her heart that it didn't mean anything. Not really. It wouldn't help her find her daddy, or it wouldn't even bring her one step closer to the desires of her heart, but this was where her father pointed. This was where he told her he was going. Tears started forming in her eyes. She didn't want to cry in front of him. She tried to hold them back, but they came anyway. Her mother saw them and put her arm around her. Grandma closed in on the other side. And Roberta felt a nudge like she had to say something.

"Thank you for buying me the binoculars."

"I did buy them for you, but that's not your gift. This is."

He stretched his arms out in both directions. The binoculars hung from her neck, and she looked at him peculiarly.

"What is?"

"This. This land. I bought it for you."

"Oh Paul," said Mother and put her hand over her mouth.

"The land?" Roberta asked.

Paul came around the front of her and knelt down. "I know what your father said about crossing the lake, and I know you wanted to feel what it was like on the other side. You wanted to get closer to him. To follow him. Because you love him and miss him. So I wanted to give you something. A place to remember him by. I'll bring you here anytime you want. It's yours. It's legally yours on your eighteenth birthday. I thought it was important that you have a place just for you and your dad."

She froze for a second, but before long, she

leaped into her step-father's arms and mouthed several thank-yous through her airy cry. Grandma and Mother hugged each other, tears streaming down their faces. Roberta pulled away and walked toward the lake. She stood on the edge and picked up a twig and twirled it into the water. It swirled slowly along the surface. Her eyes glanced up to the middle of the lake. She remembered what it was like to be on the skates and to fall through. She glanced to her right and saw the lake disappear around a bend with a tall hill on the far side. She wondered if the bend hid the canyon from her sight. She not only made it to the other side of the lake, she now owned it.

She turned around towards the three watching her in silence from the rear. She panted loudly, words and memories and thoughts sifting through her mind. She thought of her father on the real other side—the war, the far-off place she would never see. But she felt closer like he was there after all, since she had finally arrived. As she carried him here in her heart, so he came. So he lived. It was his ground, not hers, and she had to make sure it would always be that way.

"I would like to make a cross and place it in the ground. Can we?"

Her mother covered her face and nodded swiftly. Yes. They all agreed.

Paul walked up the slope to the car to get some tools. He instructed Roberta to find the right branches. They would do it together, at that moment, without delay.

She found two sturdy branches. Grandma and Mother helped her break off small twigs until Paul returned with a shovel, a mallet, a knife, and a roll of rope. They sliced the branches clean. Paul broke a large one in half to make it manageable to get into the ground, which luckily still wasn't frozen solid. He dug a small hole then pounded the piece of wood with the mallet, a slow process. Even Roberta tried a few hits. Within five minutes, Paul pronounced it sturdy enough and packed the remaining dirt around it. The other branch was smaller, and Roberta helped him wrap the rope around all four corners of the intersection between the two pieces. He tied it off and stepped away. A perfectly placed cross sat off the shore of the lake about fifteen feet. They circled around it and without warning, purged the thoughts from their minds.

"Daniel, you were a wonderful husband to my daughter and a loving father to my granddaughter. I was so proud to be your mother-in-law. You are missed."

"Dear Daniel. We have been friends for so long. You taught me everything. I wanted to fly planes because of you, because of your enthusiasm. You were so skilled. I never thought I'd ever be blessed to be here in your place. I know it's not right. I wish it wasn't so. I'd give up everything for you to be here with your family." Paul choked up, joining the tears of the others. "But rest in peace. Know that I will honor your memory by taking care of them and loving them. I miss you, my brother."

Mother sobbed, but that didn't stop her. "My dear Daniel, I'm so proud of you. You never hesitated when duty called, whether your family or your country. It's hard. It's been hard, but I know what you would want for us. You are always in our hearts and minds. Everyday. Every minute. Every second. Goodbye, my sweetheart."

Roberta dropped to her knees and placed her hands on both sides of the horizontal part of the cross. "Dear Daddy, I will visit you here, all right? And we will talk. I'll bring my airplane so you can see me fly it, and we'll watch the lake together, and see the butterflies soar into the sky. I love you, Daddy."

She leaned over and kissed the cross, then unpinned the wings from her coat and attached them to the rope holding the cross together. She stood to her feet and ran to Paul and gave him another hug.

"You're freezing," said Paul, looking at her ruddy red skin. "Let's go home. I'll bring you back here tomorrow if you like."

Roberta nodded, and the four walked up the slope. From the top, Roberta turned one last time to see the cross sitting alone by the edge of the lake. They descended the bank to the car. Paul helped all of them over the small ridge of the bank, even Roberta. They all were silent.

The car retraced its tracks. Roberta had switched seats with Grandma, so she could watch the lake fade in and out view.

"Did you mean it?" she asked.

"Who are you talking to," asked her mother.

"Father figure."

Mother smiled. She tapped Paul on the right shoulder, and he glanced back at Roberta in the backseat.

"Did I mean what?"

"Did you buy that land for me?"

"Yes. Maybe someday you could build a house for yourself there."

"A house for us." Everyone smiled. "Me and Daddy."

Paul nodded. "He would like that very much."

They rounded the edge of the lake and drove the last few miles into town. They passed

Winston Street again.

"Mom, I'm sorry I sold your ring."

"It's alright, sweetheart."

"And I'm sorry I burned the letters."

Her mother reached behind her and grabbed Roberta's hands and they clasped onto each other for a moment. As they drove past the Gulf Station, she thought again of the map on the wall.

"Paul, thank you for saving me."

"You're welcome."

Grandma patted the girl's thigh and smiled at her. "It's been quite a year, and you're growing up to be a fine young lady."

"I'm gonna fly airplanes one day."

"Is that right?"

As they pulled into the driveway, Roberta noticed Mr. Goodwin's truck parked on the right near the shed. Paul pulled up beside him.

"What's Mr. Goodwin doing here?" Roberta asked.

"I don't know," Mother said, eyes focused out the right window.

"I asked him to come," Paul said.

"Why?"

"I needed his help with something. Everyone, out of the car."

"Paul, what's this all about?"

"You'll see."

Mr. Goodwin opened the truck door and stepped out into the cold. He had a smile on his face.

"Sorry, Thaddeaus, for making you wait."

"Not at all. I haven't been here very long."

The five of them had created a circle between the two vehicles. Roberta stood to Mr. Goodwin's left.

"So, do you have it?" Paul asked.

"I sure do. But I'm a little confused who it's for. Could you point me in the right direction? Is it for Mrs. Newsom?" He smiled.

"What?" Grandma questioned.

"No, no. Not her."

"How about Mrs. Ares? Is it for her?" Paul and Mr. Goodwin played a contrived cat and mouse game that perplexed Roberta.

"No, definitely not her."

"Paul, what's going on?" asked Mother.

"So then it leaves just this young lady." Mr. Goodwin looked down at Roberta. He had a face-wide grin. "Oh, and my manners, I forgot to say 'Merry Christmas.'"

Everyone echoed the sentiment.

"So you have it in your cab?" asked Paul.

"Sure do."

"What is it?" Roberta's patience had given way to a burning curiosity. She got onto her tiptoes and glanced through the cab's back window to see if that would afford her any additional clues. It didn't.

"Well, then. Let's see what we have."

Mr. Goodwin opened the cab door and leaned across the seat, pulling back a basket with a wool blanket inside. He held it with both hands, squatted over towards Roberta, and rested it on his left knee.

"Open it."

Roberta didn't allow herself to guess or wonder. She would discover with the lift of the blanket's edge. As she turned up the flap of the blanket, she saw it and froze for a second. She thought how silly she had been this past week, announcing to the world she didn't want a gift. And now she had a pair of binoculars, and a piece of land with father's cross on it. Her heart overflowed with satisfaction, yet she looked at it, something that would complete the circle, would usher in a new year and perhaps a new era in the family.

"I thought you should have it," said Paul, "… and Mr. Goodwin was very eager to help me search out the right one for you."

"It was only right. I wouldn't have wanted it any other way," he said.

Mother and Grandma held each other's arms

and couldn't hold back the tears as Roberta reached in and removed the puppy from the basket. It yipped once, and she hugged it, cradling it under her chin.

"It looks like baby Trigger!" she exclaimed.

"A terrier. She's all yours."

Roberta looked down at the dog, now squirming. It jumped out of her arms and ran to the edge of the car. Roberta ran after it. It stopped and ran back towards her, and she knelt in the snow to play with the vibrant pup. She scooped it up into her arms and ran back to the four, stopping at Paul and giving him a hug. She did the same to Mr. Goodwin while thanking them both.

"What are you going to name her?" asked Mother.

She didn't hesitate. "Ginger." She looked at her grandma.

Grandma smiled. "Perfect. Certainly a Christmas we will never forget."

"I'm going to go introduce her to Trigger."

Mr. Goodwin shook hands with the adults and said goodbye. Roberta placed the puppy on top of Trigger's rock and explained to Ginger everything she needed to know. "Ginger, Trigger is like your father figure. You'll need to respect him. All right?"

The dog barked as if it understood, and they all went into the house with much to discuss and presents still to open.

***

By mid-afternoon, Roberta had wiped-out Ginger from hours of non-stop playing. The dog fell asleep near the fireplace, and Roberta decided to go outside with her new pair of binoculars.

"Patty!" She called to her neighbor, who pulled a new sled in the newly fallen snow. "Did you get a new sled?"

"Yes."

"What did you get?"

"A puppy."

"Where is it?"

"It's sleeping inside. I'll show you later. But look, I also got a pair of binoculars."

"Oh, can I try them?"

"Sure. Let's go play down by the lake and see what we can see. Oh, and we can look at the land I own."

"You own land?"

"I sure do. Come on. I'll tell you all about it."

"Here, let's ride on my sled together down the slope."

Roberta jumped on behind Patty, and the two

careened down the bank, flying into the snow and laughing without a care in the world.

Chapter 24

Roberta's Epilogue

Years have passed since I watched those two uniforms walk onto our front porch on Christmas Eve, 1944. Even three decades later, that image is never more than a moment away in my mind. My entire life has been shaped by that moment—both good and bad. Such a thought demands pause—how can good come from unbearable pain? It just does, and yet the good moments are fragilely framed against the backdrop of tragedy. Life may not begin this way, but it always ends so.

I decided to tell you the rest of my story using my own voice. Paul and I came to an understanding. His Christmas gift did much to soften my heart towards him, but it really took years for me to look on him to be more than a father figure. When I turned fifteen, I realized that as much as I hated to admit it, he was my father, and I loved him. I also realized I had enough love in my heart for both men. Paul was there when I went to prom and when I graduated from high school. He counseled me on my college choice—

knowing what I wanted to study. He even used his army connections to help me on my way. He loved me.

I graduated from aviation school in 1957. Paul was there to congratulate me, as was Mom and Grandma. Grandma died a little more than a year after that in early 1959. We interred her beside Grandpa Newsom. Ginger died shortly after that the same year. I buried her myself on the land across the lake.

Upon graduation, I became one of the first female pilots in the region. I wore the wings given to me by the airmen in 1944 on my uniform to remember my daddy. I still call him that. Paul is Dad.

I married a wonderful man in 1962. We lived out of state for several years as I flew planes for two of the major airlines, but I never lost sight of what I ultimately wanted to do with my life. In 1970, with my husband in agreement, we moved back home and started building a house across the lake. We moved into it in 1971, right before Paul died of a heart-attack. My mother handled his death well, and we buried him in a plot not far from Grandma and Grandpa. When our house was finished, Mother sold my childhood home and moved in with us on the lake.

I had two children of my own, and they grew

up hearing about the stories of my childhood, especially the year leading up to Christmas '45. I wanted them to hear about my doubts, my questions, and my pain. I wanted them to know that life won't always turn out the way we anticipated. I encouraged them to never be satisfied with an answer that felt wrong. Ask. Probe. And always keep moving forward. I wanted them to know that tragedy made me who I am—made me into the mother they had to deal with—good or bad. While I would have given everything back to have had my father in my life, I came to realize that everything I do have is from him, because of his sacrifice. In turn, my kids owe him the same amount of gratitude I do, even though he's only a grainy image to them.

I mounted a permanent telescope on the deck of our new house overlooking the lake. We use it to peer back across time and see the other side as clearly as if we were standing there ourselves long ago. My kids like to use the telescope to play imaginary games. But I use it to this day to remember my roots and remember the person I was once when life was still an open promise.

The original wooden cross which Paul and I built lasted no more than a year. He helped me replace it with a sturdier wooden one the following year, and it lasted through high school.

I replaced it from time to time until I eventually built a permanent one made of stone. That same year, I had Trigger's rock transported to the new location and the two memorials stand side-by-side to this day.

Mother died last year in 1974. She rests eternally beside Paul.

Over the years, I researched my father's death and finally received some answers. His plane went down in a Belgian field. Not from enemy fire but from some sort of engine malfunction. No one was ever able to determine why he wasn't able to eject himself. Last month, I traveled there and found the site—or at least the closest location I could find using my sketchy research. I said goodbye to him one last time and placed my childhood wooden airplane on the ground. It felt right. I had made it across the lake after all these years. I could finally imagine what it felt like to be drifting from the sky, knowing you'll never see those you love again. I was lucky to be there, to have survived my own lake. In retrospect, I realize that in '45, I really had made it across the lake. I just didn't know it.

THE END

A Note from the Author - If you enjoyed this story, please consider leaving a review online. (Amazon, Goodreads, Bookbub, etc…) This will enable others to find this story as well. Thank you for reading. - MWS

Other Christmas stories from Mark W Sasse:

If Love is a Crime: A Christmas Story
In 1850, a desperate runaway slave comes across a cabin in the woods that is filled with a heap of biscuits and a whole lot of love.

Christmas in the Trenches, 1914
Inspired by the true to life story.

Jolly Old St. Hick
Two city elites get stuck in the boondocks on Christmas Eve and clash with a jolly old hick.

<u>Other Novels by Mark W. Sasse</u>

A DIAMOND FOR HER: Myths & Tales of the Winasook Iron Horses Book 1
THE LOST LINEUP: Myths & Tales of the Winasook Iron Horses Book 2

THE FORGOTTEN CHILD TRILOGY
- Book 1 - A Man Too Old for a Place Too Far
- Book 2 - The African Connection
- Book 3 - A Parting in the Sky

MOSES THE SINGER - Finalist - YA Novel of the Year 2021 - TheKindleBookReview.com

A LOVE STORY FOR A NATION
THE REACH OF THE BANYAN TREE
WHICH HALF DAVID
THE RECLUSE STORYTELLER
BEAUTY RISING